AN IL

GEORGES DE LYS (1855-1931) was the pseudonym of Georges Fontaine de Bonnerive. He was in service when he published all of his early work, which included three poetry collections, beginning with *Les Idoles* (1884) and one naturalistic novel, *Raymond Meyreuil* (1886), before he published *Une Idyll à Sedôm* (1889). He went on to publish *Penthesilea* (1896), and numerous other novels, volumes of poetry and military studies, but little attention has been paid to him by orthodox literary historians, perhaps partly because the violent eroticism of the *Une Idyll à Sedôm* cast a shadow over his reputation from which it never entirely recovered, in spite of two of his subsequent works being awarded prizes by the Académie française.

BRIAN STABLEFORD'S scholarly work includes *New Atlantis: A Narrative History of Scientific Romance* (Wildside Press, 2016), *The Plurality of Imaginary Worlds: The Evolution of French roman scientifique* (Black Coat Press, 2017) and *Tales of Enchantment and Disenchantment: A History of Faerie* (Black Coat Press, 2019). In support of the latter projects he has translated more than a hundred volumes of *roman scientifique* and more than twenty volumes of *contes de fées* into English.

GEORGES DE LYS

AN IDYLL IN SODOM

TRANSLATED AND WITH AN INTRODUCTION BY

BRIAN STABLEFORD

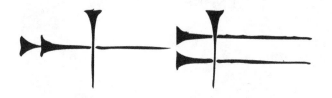

THIS IS A SNUGGLY BOOK

ISBN: 978-1-64525-057-9

CONTENTS

INTRODUCTION

UNE IDYLLE À SEDÔM by "Georges de Lys" (Georges Fontaine de Bonnerive, 1855-1931), here translated as *An Idyll in Sodom*, was first published in Paris in 1889 by Camille Dalou. A feuilleton serialization began in the literary supplement of *La Lanterne* on 23 August 1891. The novella was reprinted in 1901 by Offenstadt frères, without the author's dedication and introduction, as *La Vierge de Sedôm*, in a notable series of pretentious erotica, the Collection Orchidée.

Une Idylle à Sedôm is a significant contribution to a subgenre of French Romantic fiction consisting of lush representations of *"moeurs antiques"* [ancient mores]. The subgenre enjoyed a spectacular boom when Pierre Louÿs' *Aphrodite, moeurs antiques* (1896) became the best-selling French novel of the 1890s, launching a bandwagon on to which numerous writers and publishers were quick to jump. The origins of the subgenre went back to a cluster of *nouvelles* by Théophile Gautier, most famously "Une Nuit de Cléopâtre" (1838) and a spectacular landmark was established by Gustave Flaubert's *Salammbô* (1862). Georges de Lys was one of a group of neo-Romantic writers inspired in part by those examples—*Une Idylle à Sedôm* is dedicated to Flaubert—to carry the subgenre forward before Louÿs prompted the deluge. Other notable near-contemporary examples included Jean Lombard's *L'Agonie* (1888), Anatole France's *Thaïs* (1890) and *Cléopâtre* (1891) by Jean Bertheroy (Berthe Le Barillier).

Although the exemplars provided by Gautier and Flaubert contain considerable doses of discreet eroticism, the writers who took up the torch in the *fin-de-siècle* generally put a heavier and more explicit emphasis on that element; although it was Louÿs who brought it to the fore most elegantly and most pretentiously, *Une Idylle à Sedôm* deserves recognition for doing so in a remarkably extravagant and forthright fashion. It is unsurprising that the author felt the needed to add an apologetic introduction to the first edition of his work denying that it was pornographic, but it would also be unsurprising if many of its original readers were unable to agree.

The text of the first edition of the work concludes with a note recording that it was written in two stages, in 1885 and 1888. It is possible that those dates refer to two complete drafts, but it is more probable that the novel was abandoned part-way through and then taken up again after a pause. It might or might not be a coincidence that within that interim a *nouvelle* entitled *La Pudeur de Sodom* (1888; tr. as *The Modesty of Sodom*) by Gustave Guiches was published in *La Revue indépendante*, and swiftly reprinted as a small book, which gained a rapid notoriety; it is conceivable that the *succès de scandale* achieved by that story was what emboldened Georges de Lys to finish his novella and Camille Dalou to publish it. It is possible that Lys had not intended the Voice of the Lord to play such a flamboyant role in his story, until he took heart from Guiches' recklessness in the deployment of the device.

Georges Fontaine de Bonnerive—the aristocratic surname was his mother's, his father being plain Jean Fontaine—enrolled in the École de St-Cyr, France's military academy, in 1874, and embarked upon a long military career, attaining the rank of captain in a line regiment. He was in service when he published all of his early work, which included three poetry collections, beginning with *Les Idoles* (1884) and one naturalistic novel,

Raymond Meyreuil (1886), before he published *Une Idyll à Sedôm.* The latter was swiftly followed by another novel. *L'Enclos des cerisiers* (1890). He went on to publish numerous novels, volumes of poetry and military studies, but little attention has been paid to him by orthodox literary historians, perhaps partly because the violent eroticism of the present work cast a shadow over his reputation from which it never entirely recovered, in spite of two of his subsequent works being awarded prizes by the Académie française.

Fontaine de Bonnerive became a chevalier de la Légion d'honneur in 1898, while he was still in military service, partly because of his literary endeavors. He did some work in collaboration, notably *L'Arantelle, roman d'art* (1908), with André Ibels (1872-1932), one of the founders of the *Revue Anarchiste*, who had published an irreverent Biblical fantasy of his own, *Gamliel, Une Orgie au temps de Jésus* (Offenstadt frères, 1899). He was not the first soldier to turn his hand to literature with some success, having been preceded by Antoine-Louis Duclaux de l'Estoille (1835-1894), who published his early work during the Second Empire under the pseudonym "Louis de Lyvron." Estoille was also forgotten by orthodox literary history, but contributed slightly to that neglect by changing his signature part-way through his career, replacing his pseudonym with "A. de l'Estoille" after his life and writing were drastically interrupted by the Franco-Prussian War and the devastation of Napoléon III's Empire—a traumatic interlude which changed the attitude of his work considerably. Georges de Lys avoided any such disruption, only enlisting when the Franco-Prussian War was over and completing his entire service under the Third Republic, in the interim between the major conflicts of 1870-71 and 1914-18.

There is a certain oddity in an army officer writing neo-Romantic fiction of a kind that came to be called "Decadent," although that terminology was of very recent coinage when Georges de Lys began penning *Une Idylle à Sedôm*. The eccentricity was continued following his retirement from military service; his association with Ibels and the *Revue Anarchiste* would certainly have raised eyebrows had he still been in uniform at that time. Although the central character of *Salammbô* is a mercenary soldier, Flaubert had no military experience and was as un-military a man as could be imagined—something that must have been apparent to Fontaine de Bonnerive when he read the novel. *Une Idylle à Sedôm* is markedly different in its manner, and chooses for its protagonist the heroic victor of a crucial battle between the Hebrews and the Elamites.

It is arguable that the entire subgenre of *romans de moeurs antiques* tends to the effete, although it is not short of images of male beauty, and *Une Idylle à Sedôm* is unusual in its robust approach to plotting. The story does, however, illustrate the near-paradoxicality of the idea of a soldierly Decadent fantasy, in the orchestration of its conclusion, when its hero comes to resemble a shorn Samson who cannot recover his strength, unable to lift a finger to bring the heathen temple down or even to run away with his inamorata. That strange tension within the story is, however, an intriguing addition to its unique musculature, and adds to the interest of the work as a specimen.

Ever a literary maverick, Georges de Lys published several other studies of *moeurs antiques* in the course of his long career, including a notable novella featuring the queen of the Amazons who fought in the Trojan War, "Penthesilée" (1896; tr. as *Penthesilea*), but none equaled the extravagance and adventurous spirit of *Une Idylle à Sedôm*. Once *Aphrodite* had set a new precedent and the floodgates opened, the orgiastic excesses featured in the novella became almost commonplace, but Georges de Lys not only got there first, but proceeded with a bellicosity that his successors found difficult to match, and he deserves to be reckoned an important pioneer in the context of the Decadent Movement of the *fin-de-siècle*.

This translation was made from the copy of the Dalou edition reproduced on the Bibliothèque Nationale website *gallica*.

—Brian Stableford, April 2020

AN IDYLL IN SODOM

AUTHOR'S INTRODUCTION

A N IDYLL IN SODOM! An alarming title that will doubtless give rise to cries of immorality, scandal and, let us say the word, pornography. I foresee my poor book being signaled to public outrage and—who, knows?—perhaps even being deferred to the courts, the law is so disconcerting and human stupidity so immeasurable, and, in sum, being confused with the library of brochures of brothels and urinals.

No matter; I shall not hesitate to publish it.

I shall not hesitate, because I am conscious of the goal glimpsed, the effort attempted, and above all the artistic ideal pursued, of which *An Idyll in Sodom* is the result. Our epoch has built on the ruins of Romanticism—if they are ruins—a number of new schools. The mere word "school" reeks of pedagogy and, in consequence, smells bad. In sum, those pretended ruins are diabolically solid, since they serve as the foundations of *La Faute de l'abbé Mouret, Germinal* and so many other masterpieces,[1] but that is only a parenthetical remark.

It is admitted by any logical and independent mind that the distinction between foundation and form is a puerility. An idea is translated by words, those words form and are the sentence. If the latter is poor, or even mediocre, it renders the idea imperfectly; if the idea is rendered precisely, in a perceptible and ineluctable fashion, the sentence is good. That is the whole theory of art.

In works of the imagination, it was once believed that one had all the licenses of fantasy; that was the chink in the armor through which Romanticism was fatally wounded, in its procedure—for from the viewpoint of its foundation it remained standing.

In sum, what is Romanticism? A grandiose conception of things. What is Naturalism? An exact observation of facts. Those two pretended enemies are far from being irreconcilable; one is even astonished, on studying modern literature at close range, to see them so frequently marching forward abreast, like two oxen harnessed to

---

1 The two novels cited, by Émile Zola, were published in 1875 and 1885 respectively.

the same yoke. I cited Zola just now; Flaubert remains an even more irrefutable example. I shall not insist on that point, which Paul Bourget has elucidated so clearly in his *Essais de psychologie contemporaine*,[1] but I shall depart from there to go further by affirming that without Romanticism there could not be fabulation, or even history.

The self, so formally proscribed, is imposed on the psychology of a book as well as its style. We can only paint in accordance with our personal vision; our most exact observation is still ours, and can never be general, much less impersonal. Let us disguise that self, by all means, but let us not go so far as to deny it. So much for psychology.

What about style? I return to the theory exposed above; the idea is validated by the sentence, the sentence lives in the idea. Every laborer can arrive, if he is intelligent, in expressing his thought exactly and rendering it palpable to all; that is talent; a few can impose it and infuse it in the soul of the reader, make it his simply by means of the procedures of style; that is genius.

I therefore claim, for every artist, the right to approach no matter what subject, provided that he treats it without prejudice, without contravening the observations of science—something un-

---

1 The volume cited was first published in 1883,

fortunately forgotten by the rank and file of the Romantic school, and I proclaim that he has the right, and even the duty, to retrace the facts as he sees them and as he feels them.

In the matter of factual exactitude, the most curious thing is that the pages for which I shall be most reproached are precisely those that derive from the very source, from the Bible; for in modern criticism, Panurge is led in tow by his sheep—or, if you prefer, it is the subscribers who lead the press.

In consequence, a writer can wear away his evenings in arduous study, pursue the slightest document from library to library and impose upon himself difficult labors that serve solely to engender a single book; he can collect, with the joy of an archeologist, the smallest vestiges of primitive civilizations in fabulous times; he can be haunted by the desire—the chimera, if you wish—to resuscitate a dead, almost unknown, epoch; he can strive to overcome ever-renascent difficulties, to fray a path through collapsed tunnels, and when, bruised, pale, scratched and weary, he brings out the result of his patient effort—which might be a monument or an abortion, the effort is there regardless—his contemporaries will take his book, underline its sincere pages with lewd sniggers, content themselves with vivid depictions that their dirty imagination will make vicious, and, having emerged from the study where they went moldy, posing as moralists, they will dare to castigate the result of that patient, sincere effort, respectable by virtue of that alone, and great by virtue of that alone!

Bourgeois prudishness makes strange compromises. In the evening, after dinner, while the women are sniping at one another in the drawing room, the sated men in the smoking room facilitate their digestion by the joyful exchange of lewd jokes, not to say stupid and brutal obscenities, and vent their spleen. However, if a writer careful of his dignity has the audacity to depict faithfully, while leaving phraseology the care of covering the obligatory nudities of his scene, those same men, in speaking of his book, will abuse it, calling it pornography!

Pornography! That stupid word is exasperating. The only shameful works are the adulterated products of an obscene publicity. But who would dare to call shameful a work based on history, science and the Bible?

Pornography, the great and holy Bible? Open all its pages; read the story of Judah and his daughter-in-law Tamar, the wife of Onan, Onan himself;[1] pass on to the other Tamar who was violated by her brother Amnon, son of David; you

---

1 cf *Genesis* 38.

will see there that the cousin Jonadab, who served as the procurer, is called a very prudent friend (II *Kings*, 13:3).[1] Do you think that a historian is shocked by that? Not at all. Better still: "David was afflicted by that incest but he did not want to sadden Amnon his son, because he loved him, being his eldest." (ibid, 21).[2]

Damn! Holy King David!

Well, David was of his time; certainly, if he were resuscitated, he would be quite astonished by the reprobation of an epoch that enriches *Baronnes d'Ange*.[3]

And what about Raab the courtesan,[4] and the Levite of Gabaa,[5] the incest of Lot's daughters

---

1 This reference is incorrect, it should be to II *Samuel* 13:3; the Authorized Version describes Jonadab as a friend and a "very subtil man."

2 The A.V. only says that David was "very wroth."

3 "Baronne d'Ange" was a pseudonym adopted by more than one actual Parisian prostitute after being employed by Alexandre Dumas *fils* for a character in *Le Demi-monde* (1855). The term is used in the plural to denote pretentious whores by other writers of the period, including Marcel Proust.

4 This character, more usually rendered Rahab or Rachab, is called a prostitute in most versions of *Joshua* 2:1, but the description is challenged in other texts. The catalogue of the Bibliothèque Nationale records that George de Lys published a volume in the Offenstadt frères' Collection Orchidée series entitled *En Volupté; Rahab la Courtisane* in 1902, immediately after their edition of *Une Idylle à Sedôm*.

5 cf *Judges* 20:4-6; the place cited is rendered Gibeah in the A.V.

and the rape of Dinah![1] Let us therefore send the authors of the Bible to prison!

In the epoch of my story I find Abraham, the great patriarch, prostituting his wife Saraï twice, to the pharaoh of Egypt and to Abimelech; I see the people of Sodom wanting to abuse the angels given hospitality by Lot, and he offering the virginity of his daughters to appease the debauchees—and the latter, lacking men after the catastrophe, getting their father drunk in order to lie with him. I could multiply these examples endlessly.

Brave men, you lower your hypocritical eyes while looking down, or veil them with your splayed fingers. On the contrary, open them wide; it is healthy to study the origins of the human race, to analyze the progressive march of civilizations, the development of mores, the birth and spread of the moral and social prejudices that are now the basis of our sentiments and our laws. Why rail against an order of things fatal to the first steps of a race, instead of admiring their native simplicity and unassailable good faith?

It is necessary above all to extract important information from them. The crimes of the accursed cities have left in human memory an impression of supernatural horror; look around you, lift the veils that mask our lepers, and we are forced to

_____

1 cf *Genesis* 34.

recognize that the generations have succeeded one another without ameliorating human beings. In olden times vice was no more widespread than in our day, but it was brutally displayed; among us, it hides away hypocritically. Has Paris any fornication to envy Sodom?

Today Onan is called *Charlot s'amuse*; Sappho is depicted in *Deux Amies* and found in nature among the most intelligent of our women, Georges Sand and the Princess de Beljiososo to name but two.[1] The profligacies of Sodom are displayed in the newspapers under the headlines *Scandales d'Auch* or *Débauches du bois de Vincennes*. The *Pall Mall Gazette* is more explicit than the Bible. The *Gazette des Tribunaux* informs me that the daughters of Lot no longer have any need to get

---

1 *Charlot s'amuse* (1883) and *Deux amies* (1885) are novels by Paul Bonnetain and René Maizeroy respectively; the latter was successfully prosecuted for obscenity. The other two references are presumably to George Sand (1804-1876) and Cristina Belgiojoso (1808-1871), whose names might by misrendered deliberately. The latter was a writer and Italian revolutionary forced to flee to Paris, where she established a famous salon in the 1830s, attended by Honoré de Balzac, Victor Hugo and other pillars of French Romanticism; it was Balzac who publicized rumors of her lesbianism, which were never substantiated, any more than Baudelaire's catty allegations regarding Sand's lesbianism. The author could easily have named lesbians prominent on the contemporary Parisian social scene, but presumably refrained for diplomatic reasons.

their father drunk in order for him to make them pregnant; the incest of Tamar and Amnon is less licentious than *Zo'har*;[1] fundamentally, it is still the same.

I shall now pass on to the book itself. The ignorant will reproach me for the abuse of antique terms; conversely, scholars will accuse me of anachronisms of expression or a lack of exactitude on certain points. I shall explain myself immediately.

I have only employed Hebraic or Syriac terms in rare cases, for the sake of decorum or colorful effect, I could hardly translate *bethoulim* except by a circumlocution that would have been anachronistic and implausible in dialogue; although one has the right to speak in French of *La Pucelle* one scarcely has that of depicting her estate by the substantive derived therefrom[2] . . . I cite that example among many.

The erudite will reproach me for anachronism in using such terms as *evangelical*, in the sense of

1 *Zo'har* (1886) is a novel by Catulle Mendès.
2 *Bethoulim* is the Hebrew term for virginity. *La Pucelle* [the Maid (of Orléans)] was the nickname by which Jeanne d'Arc was commonly known in France, and was therefore acceptable in conventional literary usage, whereas *pucelage* [maidenhead] was not, having been tainted by its prolific salacious employment in eighteenth-century *romans libertins*, including those of the Marquis de Sade.

"good news," *oarystis, théories* [processions] and others of Greek etymology. I will make the observation that I have banished them from the dialogue, but that in describing on my own account, at the present moment, I believe I have a right as narrator to employ terms that are familiar to us. Electricity, for example, was not known then, but it existed and was manifest in lightning; I have therefore made use of the term electrified.

I shall not insist further on these matters of detail; I shall proceed to the gravest objection that might be raised. I have fused into one the two exiles of Agar,[1] that recounted in *Genesis* 16:1-6 and that of chapter 21:9-11, 14 & 20. I was led to that by the necessity of condensing my story, to avoid the delay of a lapse of several years. The same reason caused me to bring the destruction of Sodom closer to its deliverance. That double distortion of the Bible only alters two points of detail, precipitating events without modifying them. Has a writer the right to that license? I believe so; in any case, there are no others to reproach.

---

1 Hagar in the A.V.; although I have rendered some of the names used by the author in their more familiar English versions—including the replacement of Sedôm by Sodom—I have usually left them as he renders them, retaining Iarden [Jordan] and Gamora [Gomorrah]; I have added explanatory footnotes where it seemed useful to do so.

In conclusion, I shall arrive at the very foundation of the study. Against the enormous and somber backcloth of the capital of the fornicating cities, serving as an altar, I have attempted to make the naïve amour shine of two pure souls, two primitive individuals. That amour could not be molded by the artificial conventions of our civilization; in early times passion had as its immediate goal its sexual manifestation; it followed natural laws without prevarication or sentimentalism, and that is what enables its pure beauty. The idyll of Longus is one of the most palpable demonstrations of that.

I have, therefore, exhumed the abominations of Sodom with the sole objective of making the amour of two noble, simple, immaculate beings more sublime and more radiant; it seems to me that it would be inappropriate to accuse me of unhealthy tendencies and a depraved mentality. On the contrary, I have striven, in these pages, only to glorify natural law and to exalt it to the point of apotheosis. Amour is disappearing, and I wanted to render a throne to the dispossessed monarch!

Georges de Lys.

I

BLEAK and heavy, like a livid cloud encircling the horizon, consternation floated over Sodom. Old men, women and children were gathering in groups in the streets, and their sobs accompanied, like a dying chant, the shrill lamentations that despair extracted in spasms from their contracted throats.

A dull rumor of multiple trailing footfalls rose from the paving stones, filling the air with lugubrious echoes; and the clamor increased, like a swell inflating waves devouring a strand: like a rising tide, the population of Sodom, save for the able-bodied men who had rallied to the debris of the troops of King Bara, the leader of the army of the Pentapolis, was descending from the mountain and spreading out into the city sacked by the Elamites.

A vast field of desolation, Sodom's breached walls were disemboweled, its gaping gates broken down, the dislocated timbers dangling miserably from twisted bronzed hinges. In the streets and the squares, the *teraphim*,[1] tipped from their pedestals, strewed the ground with formless debris that the victorious soldiers had taken pleasure in mutilating. Here and here, fire had completed the work of the invaders; devastated families were contemplating the smoking rubble of their homes in impotent rage. The palace and temples, above all, had been subjected to the covetousness of the enemy and testified to the savagery of the pillage.

The Elamites had burned the doors of cedarwood in order to tear away more easily the sheets of silver garnishing the joints; the porphyry baths and onyx basins were chipped and soiled with filth; the stout colonnades, and granite steles had collapsed, felled by the blows of sledgehammers.

Shittim wood panels, torn apart or half-consumed, were plastering the unveiled nudity if the walls lamentably. And in the temple of Nabou,[2] the

---

1 The precise significance of the Biblical term *teraphim* remains a trifle controversial; it is usually translated euphemistically, as "idols" but Georges de Lys would have supposed that its specific reference was to phalluses.
2 Nabou was the spelling favored by some nineteenth-century French Assyriologists for the name of an Akkadian god otherwise rendered Nabu or Nebo. Generally considered to

tatters of the great lacerated awning were twisting in the wind like the veil of a tearful widow . . .

Sodom: Sodom the beautiful, the city of delirious orgies, through which the fiery simoom of lustful amour passed, where the song of kisses unfurled its ever-ascendant scale; Sodom, the city of crimson crowned with flowers and embalmed by amber, mingling in the same gust the aromatics of Araby and the effluvia of palpitating flesh; Sodom, superbly impure, whose name alone caused eyelids to flutter over the lowered eyelids of adolescents and fabric extend over the erect breasts of virgins; Sodom, the Ark of sensualities!

As the strident scythe of the reaper slices through the sunlit crop, without sparing the crimson poppies or the azure cornflowers, and leaves the loose stalks to fade on denuded fallow land, so the Elamite has passed over the flourishing city, strewing mourning and ruination. Then, like a torrent in victorious flood, he has swept away the harvest, and the fertile field is no longer anything but a stony chaos drowned in accumulations of mud . . .

---

be the god of writing and prophesy, he is a slightly eccentric choice as the overseer of the excesses of Sodom.

✳

And the white wave of the crowd spread out into the black city, howling its lament. Stray dogs, disturbed in their sinister feasting, growled over the cadavers, while crows, tightening the great circles of their flight, let lugubrious croaks rain down.

In the distance, in the falling dusk, the yapping of jackals and hyenas wept. Meanwhile, at the horizon, the sun was descending majestically, illuminating with its expiring splendor the charnel-house over which the final rays were causing pools of blood to oscillate.

In the outlying district of Bala stood a palace sober in ornamentation, of severe but grandiose aspect. The façade of bricks was raised over a substratum of red sandstone streaked with bitumen, obtaining daylight over an interior courtyard with white marble pacing stones. A covered gallery sustained by rectangular pedestals carved in blood-red porphyry ran around the four internal faces; in the center was a pentagonal basin, from which sprang a fount of limpid water, which, as it fell back into the pool, was vaporized into mist and diffused its freshness through the ambient atmosphere. That palace was the dwelling of the rich Lot, son of Harran, a man of property, the owner of large flocks, and the nephew of the opulent Abram, the Hebrew whose livestock populated the entire valley of Mamré.

Like the other edifices of Sodom, Lot's palace only rose by one story over a ground floor with powerful supports. The vaulted roof supported on its beams a terrace that covered the whole of the building, but without extending over the interior courtyard.

Over the arches of brick a bitumen sheet was set, furnished very pure by the wells of the Valley of Shaveh, and its impermeable crust was overladen by a bed of earth crowning the house with a suspended garden. Orange-trees, mimosas, sassafras, pomegranates and oleanders combined the perfume of their flowers and the variegated brightness of their fruits with the somber foliage of myrtles and holly and the bristling vegetation of cacti and aloes. The odorous shrubs of Araby fused their rare scents with the aromas of wild canes. Peppers and long clusters of pellitory tumbled in cascades along the walls, cutting across the bricks reddened by the forceful kiss of the sun, similar in the foliage of their creepers to the loose tresses that scatter in undulating curls over the forehead of a beautiful virgin, reddened by modesty.

After a bloody brawl between Lot's shepherds and Abram's, the uncle and the nephew had separated, by common accord. Abram was established at Kiriath-Arba; Lot had descended the Iarden as far as Sodom.

Bara, the ruler of the city, amazed by his immense flocks, the army of his pastors and the multiple riches of his entourage, had accepted the alliance offered by the Hebrew and had conceded lush pastures, woods and vineyards to him, as well as the palace in the outlying district of Bala which belonged to him.

Bara did not act without such largesse without motive or design. United in confederation with Gamora, where Bersa reigned, Adama, governed by Sennaab, and Ze'Boim, which was Ze'meber's, and finally Bala, which later became Zo'har, he had just fallen, along with his allies, under the yoke of the king of the Elamites, Koudour, a servant of the deity Lahomer.[1]

Sodom, along with the entire Pentapolis, was suffering from its subjugation and tributary charges. Its sovereign was nursing the secret thought of recovering its independence. Lot, with his shepherds and his wealth, was a force; above

---

1 In French versions of the Bible the name of this Elamite king is usually rendered as Kedorlaomer, a name alleged by etymologists to fuse *kudur* [servant] with the name of the goddess Lagamar. English versions generally prefer Chedorlaomer.

all, he was related to Abram, whose opulence and house even surpassed those of his nephew. In spite of their separation, Bara knew that their amity was unafflicted, so he considered Lot to be an important ally.

The latter eventually penetrated Bara's hopes and encouraged them—the liberation of the Pentapolis would relieve him of his part of the tribute and assure him of a greater security—but he did not make any engagement that might, in case of failure, compromise his life's work.

For twelve years Bara had prepared his revolt. It burst forth suddenly and intensively. Koudour-Lahomer, surprised by the unexpected eruption, was obliged to release his prey. The five cities of the Pentapolis were instituted as free cities.

Scarcely had a year gone by when Koudour-Lahomer reappeared, menacing. He had summoned his vassals; reinforced by the troops of Amraphel, Price of Shinnar, by the archers of Ariock, King of Ellacar and Pount, and finally by the cavalry of Thidal, the chief of the nomad tribes, he had raced into southern Syria, conquered it almost without striking a blow, and then engaged in the valley of Siddim, where he ran into the army of the Pentapolis.

The battle was fierce. To begin with, Bara was able to think that he was victorious; after being breached in their front the Elamites retreated in disorder, but at that moment Thidal, who had forded the river in an oblique maneuver, fell upon the left flank, where Sennaab was in command, cut off the Iarden, and threw him back on the troops of Sodom. Then the Elamites, profiting from the confusion sown in the enemy ranks, took the offensive again, and the defenders of the confederation were soon fleeing in all directions. They were cut to pieces; many went astray in the woods that covered the valley; there they fell prey to wild beasts or were swallowed up in the wells of bitumen that proliferated in the forests. The debris that escaped the carnage reached the mountain.

When the news spread in Sodom of the defeat suffered by Bara and the extermination of his troops in their retreat through the wooded valley, panic depopulated the city. Only a small number of citizens, among whom was Lot, continued to reside in the city. The Hebrew could not believe that the army of the Pentapolis had been completely destroyed; he still had before his eyes its devastating triumph of the previous year.

Shortly afterwards, the rumor was confirmed of the approach of the Elamites. Although shaken, Lot did not believe the peril to be imminent. While he was evacuating his flocks and burying his treasures, the emigration of the population was completed and Koudour-Lahomer entered a city that was almost deserted. He took Lot, his wife, two daughters and the personnel of his household prisoner, along with the rare inhabitants found in Sodom; he devastated and pillaged the city, kept his captives as hostages, and withdrew with an immense booty.

The people of Sodom returned to their sacked capital.

Elbows tight against his body, bulging pectorals inflating their knotty veins, breath whistling, shoulders projected forward as if advancing toward a goal, a robust bare-chested man clad only in a coarse loincloth girding his loins frayed a path through the crowd. His irresistible surge entered into the multitude like a plowshare into the soil, and his superb bearing imposed on those he shoved out of the way. He was Iabel, Lot's slave, the foremost of his oxherds. Having taken refuge on the mountain, he had seen the Elamite hordes quit Sodom; immediately, abandoning his herds, he had started running, moved by a single thought: that of discovering the fate of the master he loved.

He stopped in front of Lot's abode. In such haste during the march that had brought him, he no longer dared cross the threshold, the broken-down door of which was agape, like the bloody maw of a wild beast. At the presentiment of a disaster, his haste vanished. His muscular legs, previously so alert, wobbled under him and, suddenly yielding, let him collapse on to a heap of rubble. There, huddled with his elbows on his knees and his palms under his jaws, his terror-dilated eyes stared at the porch, which was summoning him, but which he did not have the strength to approach.

He came to his feet with a start; carried away by a sudden surge, head bowed, he found himself inside.

The din of the crowd was muffled by the massive walls; he shivered, alone in the sepulchral silence that enveloped him. The confused shadow falling from the walls penetrated him with a religious horror; nevertheless, he plunged into the dwelling. His bare feet posed on the paving stones soundlessly, as if they might have awakened echoes and troubled the peace of an ossuary.

The master's chamber was empty. The deserted gynaeceum was in a frightful disorder. In places, the whiteness of the marble bore imprints of feet and hands, written in stigmata of blood. Were his masters dead? Had they been snatched from their abode and cast, writhing, on to the sacrificial pyre? Oh, that doubt, that anguishing doubt! And Iabel despaired.

He lay down in the stone of the extinct hearth, threw the flap of his loincloth over his ash-soiled head and sank into his dolor . . .

A groan as long and sad as the sob of the wind on a winter night ululated in the darkness and died away in Iabel's ears.

The oxherd raised his head, pushed the flap of cloth aside, and listened . . .

Soon, a further plaint exhaled its expiring note. The man stood up, haggard, searching the shadows; then, rapidly, his fingers rotating a dry stick over a dead ember in the hearth, he set the scattered twigs alight, gathered them into a clump and, torch in hand, recommenced his search,

The sighs continued, more painfully, always more strangled, like the end of a death-rattle. His ears attentive, guided by them, Iabel reached the terrace. There he heard them more distinctly, punctuated by hoarse coughs.

A superstitious dread gripped him; the blood was buzzing in his brain, hammering his temples and squeezing him as if he were in the grip of an icy claw. However, he continued getting closer.

There . . . in a clump of mimosas, the crumpled leaves were creaking, the branches had quivered without a breath of wind furrowing the air. He penetrated the thicket and his torch illuminated the bronzed nudity of a body struggling in the throes of agony. He leaned over and recognized in that vague form Zirouya, a prepubescent servant girl employed in attendance on the master's daughters.

Kneeling beside her, he lifted her head, which was lolling inert on her shoulders; then the child opened her eyes and raised a grateful gaze toward Iabel. Her lips moved, but only inarticulate, guttural sounds escaped. She fell back into atony.

He would not know anything!

The oxherd took her in an embrace, and the moribund girl was soon laid down in the gynaeceum on the fleeces that served her mistresses as a bed. While cool water trickled over her temples, Iabel's mouth, stuck to hers, insufflated a vital breath. She was able to proffer a few words.

In view of her young age, the unfortunate girl had served the barbarians as a plaything. The master, his family and his servants had been taken into captivity by Koudour-Lahomer and comprised part of his booty.

The effort that Zirouya made to speak was her last. She stiffened in a supreme convulsion.

Iabel summoned neighbors and confided the care of the child's funeral to them. He took up his traveling staff, girded his loins, rubbed his limbs with oil, and headed in all haste toward the valley of Mamré, in order to reach the oak in the shelter of which Abram, Lot's uncle, had erected his tent.

II

ON palm mats strewn with soft fleeces taken from lambs that had never been previously sheared and whose wool had been dipped twice in scarlet, the son of Therah is lying. The shadow falling from the bushy foliage is filtering a vague daylight into the tent through the gap in the leather curtains.

Around the Hebrew, sitting cross-legged, are Mamré, Escol and Aner, his allies, all three Amorrheans.[1] They have assembled in council at

---

1 Abraham's alliance with these three Amorites is mentioned in passing in *Genesis* 14, on which the present story is based; although the episode related in this chapter is fictitious, it reflects mixed signals given in the Old Testament regarding the relationship between the Hebrews and the Amorites, who were eventually destroyed by Joshua, although many modern scholars think that the Israelites were ingrate descendants of the Amorites. Naphis is, of course, an invention.

the news of the incursion of the Elamites, in order to discuss the measures to be taken in the face of the peril.

In addition to the chiefs, a handsome adolescent, Naphis of Gamora, is standing behind Abram. The patriarch is fond of him, and honors him like a son. His tenderness envelops him all the more absolutely because the jealous God has refused him all legitimate posterity. For long years the beautiful Saraï has made the delights of his bed, but life has not germinated in her entrails. The child whom the Hebrew had had by her maidservant is wandering in the desert with the proud Agar; Abram would be sad and alone if he did not have Naphis.

When the young man revealed himself for the first time to the Hebrew's gaze, the patriarch bent his knee at the sight of his sunlit beauty, in ecstasy before the Kherub that Heaven had sent him. He was as beautiful as only the masculine form can be in its impeccable splendor; so, when Abram had recognized a human being in Naphis, his ravished eyes contemplated him so passionately that his image penetrated into him and filled with a new paternity the void of his isolated soul.

Disdainful of the bites of the sun and the stings of the wind, Naphis displayed his slender upper body in its free nudity. The polish of the flesh was blurred by delicate fibers that the muscles and the arteries molded under the amber skin. The speckled robe of a lynx, stifled between his hands of bronze, was knotted around his robust hips; his muscular legs were freed from it, and, leaning on the ground seemed to conquer it and imprint their seal upon it. The bearing of his head was proud and his physiognomy mild. Thick wavy hair spread over his shoulders, like the fleecy mane of a wild horse, and in that somber frame, his mouth laughed warmly and his gaze, doubling the sky, spread an amorous radiance.

He was in attendance at the council because, in spite of his youth, Abram had entrusted the governance of his pastors to him.

Already, Escol and Aner had spoken successively. Alarmed by the suddenness of the attack and the success of the invaders, they proposed to lift their tents and transport them further toward the sunset. Mamré was tormenting the long beard drowning his capacious breast indecisively when Abram spoke:

"Men, are you sons of jackals who tremble before the light? Are you women whom fear chills the blood in their veins and freezes the marrow in your bones? In making an alliance with the Amorrheans I thought them brave. Depart, then, flee! Your wealth and your flocks I shall keep; alone with my servants I shall await the enemy. Go, be wanderers and miserable all your life; the victorious Hebrew will remain master of the Amorrhean lands.

Quivering, the three men were on their feet. Aner, with fury in his eyes and foam on his mouth, was gathered on his rigid heels, clenching his fists, lowering his head like a bull about to charge with a formidable surge.

Already, though, Naphis was before Abram; his hand fell upon the powerful neck of the Amorrhean and bent him toward the ground. The patriarch made him let go and, marching upon the three brothers, imposed silence on them by the majesty of his person.

His voice resumed, louder, as imperious as the roar of a lion whose sleep has been troubled.

"Flee, disperse like dry leaves in the desert wind; flee like timid hares before the barking of hounds; I break my alliance with you; I cast down the ring that Mamré has put on my finger and I reclaim the one that he has of my amity!"

Escol and Aner, their hair bristling on the cranium and the face, showed their white teeth ferociously clenched beneath the rictus that contracted their lips. Eyes glowering, they measured their gazes with Naphis, whose arrogant composure opposed a superb challenge to them. Already, hands were grasping the hilts of daggers. Mamré, grave and impenetrable, warded off the carnage.

"Hebrew, your anger judges poorly. What you do, I will do, and my brothers with me; I have not engaged my oath in vain. However, if our amity weighs upon you, you can liberate yourself therefrom—but remember that you alone will have wanted it."

In the silence that weighed upon those words the sound of precipitate footfalls rises; the veil of the tent shivers and moves aside; Iabel, dusty and exhausted, falls at Abram's knees.

"Father and Lord, the truth comes via my mouth; will you hear your slave?"

"Speak," said the patriarch.

"Your nephew, the rich Lot, my illustrious master; the wife dear to his soul, his daughters, Zogar the flower of grace and Radja the fruit of beauty, his entire household and all his treasures are in the power of Koudour-Lahomer, who is carrying them away in his booty."

"Is this true?"

"Alas! Sent by my master to take his herds to the mountain, I found the palace devastated on my return. A dying slave informed me of the disaster; without delay I started running and I have come to you."

"Your name?"

"Iabel, chief of the son of Harran's oxherds.

"Get up; henceforth, Iabel is the name of a free man. Women," he shouted from the threshold of the tent, "wash his feet, anoint his body with aromatics; let him be clad in my most sumptuous robe and shod in my finest sandals; prepare the meal that he will eat by my side. You, Naphis, have the rallying buccinas sounded. At dawn, I depart for war."

Mamré advanced: "Our alliance is not undone; the insult that touches my friend touches me. I am with you."

Escol and Aner approached, their hands extended; the former spoke:

"Once, we only had our own property to defend; we preferred to lose it and have peace. Now, you are attacked; we will fight by your side."

Aner added: "And you shall see whether we are cowards."

All night long the bellicose appeals of the iobel have awakened echoes in the hills and great fires biting the crests, their bloody mouths laughing, have spat out the alarm. Dawn is paling, cutting out numerous shadows, the silhouettes of which stand out clearly against the gray pallor of the

Orient. From all points they are converging in a noisier and denser swarm; then the red sun rises over the world and illuminates the armed host, which gathers turbulently around the oak of Mamré.

All are there. Aner's men are mounted on Arab stallions as rapid as desert gazelles; the horses are whinnying and bucking, the horsemen brandishing their pikes, the metal of which shines in the sunlight and reflects blinding rays. Escol has brought seventy dromedaries laden with gourds and conducted by sinewy camel-drivers with long flame-hardened spears. Mamré's archers are leaning on the large bows, whose strings of woven gut they are verifying. Abram has three hundred and eighteen men with him, the elite of his shepherds, equipped with their slings; at their head stands Naphis, his hand on his broad blade.

The chariots of the chiefs line up their solid cedar-wood shafts, their wheels fully circled by bronze. Abram salutes his allies.

On a pyre of resinous wood he immolates a dozen heifers as white as milk, having never conceived; soon, the flame emits swirls of smoke that rise straight into the sky, carrying the perfume of the holocaust to God; and Abram's pastors intone a warrior hymn in honor of El-Elion.[1]

---

1 This epithet, meaning, "the Highest," and used for the

*Sing canticles to the Lord who reigns in the skies;
announce among the peoples the strength of his
name*

Hereb, Lelhoe, Zebaoth!

*Lord, you are my protector and my glory, and you
exalt my forehead; with you I have no fear of the
thousands of enemies who surround me!*

Hereb, Lelhoe, Zebaoth!

*Lord, let your hand weigh upon all your enemies,
let your law by heavy to all those who hate you!*

Hereb, Lelhoe, Zebaoth!

*You will burn them like an ardent fire by showing
them your blazing face; the wrath of the Saddhaï will
cast them into trouble and its fire will devour them!*

---

first time in *Genesis* 14, is usually rendered as El Elyon. The
formulation of the triple epithet employed in the hymn appears to be original; another epithet used therein, Saddhai,
is an eccentric rendering of Shaddai [Almighty], which is
given in its usual form elsewhere in the story and might
simply be misprinted at this point.

Hereb, Lelhoe, Zebaoth!

And we shall sing hymns to the Lord who will heap us with his benefits; we will make the air resound with the glory of the Almighty!

Hereb, Lelhoe, Zebaoth!

Abram advanced again, cutlass in hand, and sacrificed twelve more victims. He took out their entrails, heart and liver, and joined those fruits to his first offering.

While the meat was roasting, virgins and ephebes joined hands and rounded out their dances, circling the pyre on which the holocaust was consumed.

Naphis joined them, and the male beauty of the young man captivated all gazes. Naked, rubbed with cinnamon, he plied his limbs, as supple as a serpent rolling and unrolling its flexible coils. Simultaneously strong and graceful, he excited the admiration of all, and the patriarch contemplated him amorously, with pride, proud of the son that he had elected.

The Hebrew's servants withdrew the roasted quarters from their enormous skewers; they butchered the flesh and circulated it among the troops, carrying the fuming meat on vast platters cut in transversal roundels from the trunk of a centenarian chestnut tree. During the men's meal, Abram gathered his allies again and the Hebrew broke the bread and shared the salt with the three Amorrheans.

Then, gravely, the four chiefs exchanged the kiss of peace and mounted their chariots.

Abram gave the signal. The troops moved off; the campaign had begun.

While the dogs, tugging their leashes, howled mortally, the women, evoking long widowhoods of amour, watched the men draw away dejectedly. They veiled their faces and tore their hair, powdering it with dirt that their clenched hands labored and their gasping mouths chewed. Only their crippled servants were mute and pensive; they were thinking about ancient battles and following with jealous eyes those who were departing in order to vanquish.

III

A cry of delight has resuscitated Sodom; foreheads prostrated in the ashes are raised, the lamentations break off in throats in order to explode in joyful clamors; the news flies from mouth to mouth, grows and bursts forth universally: Abram has attacked the Elamites, Abram is victorious!

At Dan he has routed their army; at Hobu he has exterminated it. He is bringing back the liberated captives and recovered riches: he will soon arrive; he is awaited.

Bara, King of Sodom, appears on the threshold of his palace, a diadem on his head, in all the pomp of triumphal celebrations. Respectfully inclined, the evangelical messenger stands at his side. The prince extends his arms to him, lifts him up, and passes around his neck his necklace of beryls, sardonyxes and carbuncles, and then embraces him before the crowd, whose members stamp their feet with enthusiasm.

Triumphal arches are erected; the streets are decked with flags and strewn with branches; the breeze makes sheets of scarlet linen and crimson curtains undulate; Lot's palace is decorated with flowers and trophies; and over the flutter of bright colors the sun is flamboyant.

At the gate of Bala gigantic pyres are built; trees of aromatic species furnish their precious wood: cedar, sandalwood, thuya, further coated with stacte, galbanum, incense and odorous resins.

At the head of warriors who escaped the massacre, Bara goes to meet the Hebrew. The acclamations are redoubled as they pass by; the crowd floods the squares, spreads out in the streets, crowns the walls and overflows into the plain.

The hours of waiting go by slowly and feverishly. Sometimes cries sow expectation; necks stretch, eyes squint and heads are hoisted over the shoulders in front of them. Nothing appears yet, and the impatience is increased by the sudden disappointment.

The sun, at its zenith, pours forth its devouring ardor; a heavy acrid mist is floating over the breathless crowd when a dull rumble arrives at the anxious ears, like the distant noise of a torrent swollen by spring rain. It grows; gazes are directed toward the thick vapor rising at the horizon.

Finally, through the cloud of dust, reflections sparkle that the sun draws from the polished mirror of weapons; a dark stripe emerges, magnified into a swarming mass like an ant-hill, and gradually, the various elements of the army stand out distinctly.

First advanced the cymbalists with large copper disks, the buccinaires with twisted rams'-horns, the drummers with resounding bronze tympani, tearing the air with their strident notes, which drowned out the hubbub of the crowd, the hammering hooves of the horses and the uneven rolling if the chariots.

After them marched the sling-wielders, the thongs of woven leather wrapped around their right wrists, one arm swinging, tanned by the perpetual burn of the sun, now that it was laid bare in order to give free play to the joints. An untanned goatskin pinned under the armpit covered the other shoulder and protected the back. The waist was draped with a loincloth of coarse cloth fastened by the strap from which the sack full of rounded pebbles was suspended.

The chief of the archers appeared, standing upright on his chariot with massive wheels illuminated with cinnabar, pulled by two black bulls. Their curved horns were decorated with bloody remains. At the front of the chariot, suspended by the hair, black and grimacing, the tongue tumefied and the punctured eyes hanging out of the orbits, was the head of Thidal, the chief of the nomad tribes, killed at Hoba.

His troop followed, long oak-wood bows with slack strings over the shoulder with leather quivers full of fletched arrows, terminated by sharp fragments of flint or sharpened fish-bones. They marched at a brisk and rhythmic pace, awakening a sonorous echo that reverberated from the high walls of the enclosure.

Aner's men followed, their burnooses floating behind them like white wings, prancing on their Arab stallions. Camped on the skins of wild beasts, whose heads and claws swung menacingly, their muscular thighs stuck to the flanks of their mounts, those horsemen were brandishing their pikes in their right hands and holding the bridles of their horses with the left, the forearms of which were fitted with round shoulders made from strong onager-hide.

The camel-drivers, in woolen robes belted with hempen rope, were crouched on the humps of their dromedaries. They carried sheaves of javelins, and their left flanks were armed with a sword. During the battle the spears served them for skewering and throwing; the sword became their defense when they dismounted. A semicircular shield hung from the saddle-bow, ready to be unhooked in order to protect them.

The convoys marched in their midst: long files of carriages overflowing with reconquered riches and new booty; the litters of the liberated prisoners, Lot's hung with crimson draperies and that of his daughters veiled with linen and ornamented with hyacinth. Sometimes the curtains parted and the radiant beauty of the two virgins ignited covetousness in the eyes of the crowd.

There was an enormous surge; acclamations burst forth: the chiefs were arriving on their battle-chariots, with Abram at the head. As a supreme honor he had admitted to his side Naphis, his child of election, whose valor had forced the victory at Hoba; and the people did not know whether they ought to accord more admiration to the sublime old man or the adorable young man. One was resplendent with celestial majesty, the other dazzling with amour.

Bara was in the midst of his avengers. The King of Sodom was distinguished among them all by virtue of his tall stature and the sumptuousness of his garments. His chariot, laminated with bronze, represented the Tower of Babel at the moment of the confusion of languages. Each spoke of its wheels was a single elephant-tusk marvelously fitted into the rim by claws of sculpted gold.

Three black stallions harnessed in front, emitting hot vapor through the nostrils, ignited trails of sparks beneath their impatient feet and shook the reins furiously that Bara was holding in one hand; with the other he was leaning on his iron buckler, forged by Tubalcain himself, taken from the vestiges of Henokhia.[1]

The army spread out under the walls and stopped.

White files of virgins in linen tunics on which hyacinth blossomed, their loose hair streaming with cinnamon and their breath embalmed with myrrh advanced processionally, carrying perfumed unguents and bread and salt on iron trays.

The ephebes of the temple then unfurled the golden ribbon of their serene nudity, their bodies shiny with aromatic oils; they had golden cups and amphorae full of generous wine distilled by the hills of Arba.

The two files intersected, stopped and prostrated themselves before Abram, intoning a song composed to his glory.

---

1 Henokhia is the city that Cain is recorded as building in *Genesis* 4:17, which he named after his son Enoch; it is featured, monstrously, with the same spelling that Lys employs, in one of the *Poèmes barbares* (1862) of Charles Leconte de Lisle, which renders Cain's name as Qain, as Lys does when he refers to the city again.

Glory to the Hebrew of the valley of Mamré, glory to Abram!

He has appeared, he has fought the enemy from the height of the stars; the bow of the strong has been broken, the gods have broken their teeth in their mouths, their name has been effaced from the world for all eternity.

Glory to the Hebrew of the valley of Mamré, glory to Abram!

The horses have broken their hooves in the impetuosity of their flight; the cadavers of their masters hang in shreds from the brambles of the road.

Glory to the Hebrew of the valley of Mamré, glory to Abram!

He has put up his tent in the sun; he has emerged therefrom full of ardor to run like a giant in the lists; from one extremity of the world to the other, everything has ceded before him.

Glory to the Hebrew of the valley of Mamré, glory to Abram!

His head is also aureoled with glory, his beauty is resplendent on his luminous face, a furnace for his enemies, a sun for his allies.

Glory to the Hebrew of the valley of Mamré, glory to Abram!

Let us raise our gates to give passage to the king of glory, to the victor strong in battles; let us celebrate his imperishable memory in our songs.

Glory to the Hebrew of the valley of Mamré, glory to Abram!

Let virgins be offered to him with transports of joy, let them conceive by him in order to perpetuate his race in the succession of time, in order that peoples might publish his praise in all the centuries of centuries.

Glory to the Hebrew of the valley of Mamré, glory to Abram!

While the people in delirium repeated "Glory to the Hebrew!" Abram cried in a thunderous voice: "Glory to Elohim!"

And, uniting with his action of grace, the patriarch's warriors launched toward the firmament:

Hereb, Lelhoe, Zebaoth!

The appeals of the iobel resounded, preceding Malki-Zedeck, prince of Shalem;[1] the choirs parted before him and he came to Abram to offer him bread and wine.

Abram inclined before Malki-Zedeck, whom he knew to be a priest of the Almighty. The prince of Shalem imposed his hands on the victor's forehead, and proclaimed in a prophetic voice:

"Let Abram, the elevated father, son of Therah, issue of Shem, be blessed by Almighty God who created Heaven and Earth! El-Elion be praised, who has put your enemies in your hands! Already I have read in the stars your innumerable posterity, but the time has not yet come."

Abram replied:

"Prince, cohen of Almighty God, a tithe of the spoils belongs to you; it is due to Elohim and his servant."[2]

Bara spoke:

---

1 English Bibles usually have Melchizedek, king of Salem. Zedek was a Canaanite deity, who is fused with the god of the Hebrews in this passage.

2 Technically, a *cohen* (plural *cohanim*) was a priest of the Temple of Jerusalem, but the present text uses the term anachronistically, and much more generally, to refer to priests of various religions.

"Hebrew, you are victorious; everything is yours; keep the booty, but return my people to me."

The patriarch raised his hand.

"I swear by El-Elion, the sovereign Master, king of peoples and worlds," he proffered, "that I want none of your riches. I accept the subsistence of my army and the part due to my allies the Amorrheans, but for myself I shall not take a thread. It shall not be said that you have enriched Abram."

"So be it," said Bara, "but Abimael, high priest of Nabou, has a daughter beautiful among all virgins. Maheleth is the jewel of Sodom; I guarantee her *bethoulim*. We will bring her to you, that she might ornament your couch with her grace and her beauty. My astrologers have learned from the constellations that your posterity will govern the world; let Maheleth conceive of you; let your sons, the stock of your imperishable race, be the pledge of our eternal alliance."

At a sign from the king, Abimael had advanced, clad in his sacerdotal vestments, the splendor of which sparkled. He was conducting the veiled Maheleth by the hand. Before Abram the veil fell and the virgin appeared, blushing modestly, aureoled with light, in her adorable beauty.

Naphis was to Abram's right. His gaze sought that of Maheleth, appealed to it, and fused it with his own; and the radiance sprung from the virginal pupils gripped his heart entirely.

Meanwhile, Abram replied: "Take this virgin back to the gynaeceum; I do not want in my bed a woman engendered by a priest of your gods; I am the servant of the sole Elohim. I have under my tent the noble Saraï, who is awaiting my return; I do not want your gold or your daughters."

While Maheleth drew away, Naphis sensed his heart departing in her wake; he was still gazing when the cortege vanished under the gate of Bala, and he did not sense two avid eyes peering at him through the gaps in the litter where the captives he had delivered were lying.

It passed before him and vanished in its turn behind the walls.

He had not seen it!

Night fell. Abram established his camp at the foot of the ramparts; he refused, for himself and his people, the hospitality that was offered to him in a city vowed to the idolatrous worship of Sin and Nabou.

IV

THE city was starred by lights, as wild as the dilated pupils of felines lying in wait for their prey by night, insulting the limpid diamonds with which the firmament constellated the immaculate azure of its serene profundity. Up above, the pure clarities; down below, the bloody fires of the orgy; in the heavens, the harmonious choir of the stars, vibrant with love in their progress through the immeasurable ether; in Sodom, an atmosphere heavy with aromatics and meat, the wild exhalations of beings in rut, profane and lubricious songs and groans of lust.

On the edge of the camp, Naphis was staring irresistibly at the city. In its enormous fermenting mass, Sodom was crouching like a monstrous beast, breathing lust and sweating debauchery, its blinking eyes illuminated by hot gleams. The rumor swelling over the city was only the painful snore of its sated entrails; a troubled mist, in which the diffuse light of thousands of eyes floated, was evaporating from the sprawling body of the panting beast.

And that frightful colossus was attractive. It seemed to be pumping the ambient things and beings into it, by means of an absorbing attraction; its gaping gate sucked in Naphis, like the open maw of a snake fascinating a bird, with the pollution of its impure breath, and constraint precipitated him fatally into the extended gulf.

The young Gamoran was still hesitant. Brave in combat, he trembled before the inextricable maze through which a flood of carnal sensuality was flowing. To his innate purity, the excesses of Sodom appeared confused, sinister and unfathomable. His thought went astray in desire as if suspecting its mysteries. Amour was only known to him by way of its manifestations in nature, the coupling of the animals in his flocks. He wanted to know more, and his effort troubled him. His temples were throbbing under the tumultuous flux of blood; unfamiliar needles were disquieting his flesh; his being was unhinged under the intense vibration of his nerves. He shuddered, collapsed on the ground and closed his eyes.

An appeasement of an indescribable sweetness enveloped him, a voluptuous languor invaded his abandoned limbs and his lips palpitated in a vague kiss. A frisson shook him, and then cradled him with a delicious somnolence.

The image of Maheleth floated behind his closed eyelids. He saw the virgin again in her amber splendor, bathed in sunlight, haloed by innocence; her eyes came to his like two stars wept by the sky, softening their glare in a dust of gold; they magnified their luminous waves, melting over him, drowning his in their pupils. The erect summits of her breasts pressed into his chest; a magical breath fused with his own . . .

He threw out his arms, as if for an enlacement, shivering with an unknown happiness . . . and suddenly shook off his dream . . .

After a mute prostration, he sat up straight.

There: she was there, in that absorbing city, the Beloved, the virgin who had just divinized his ecstasy; she was there; she was summoning him!

Resolutely, he crossed the limits of the camp with a firm step and disappeared into the somber corridor, engulfed beneath its heavy vault.

He advanced between massive pillars, the thickset steles that supported the bold thrust of the basaltic arch. The dubious clarity of torches flickered in the mist of acrid smoke that padded and saturated the atmosphere with bituminous exhalations; then the firmament was resplendent again in its magnificence.

Naphis respired.

He engaged in a broad artery, without a determined goal but guided by a confused hope. Sometimes, his gait became firmer, in an elastic stride, while he went confidently toward his beloved; sometimes, it slackened, as he thought about the inanity of his search. In the depths of his heart, however, a presentiment cried out to him that amour was summoning him, and that his footsteps were leading him to Maheleth. What did the belated hour matter, or the implausibility of a nocturnal emergence of the daughter of the high priest? He wanted to see her again, and his exasperated desire almost created a certainty for him.

Naphis stopped, indecisively, in the main square of the Pentapolis. It formed a regular pentagon bordered by palaces, and its angles were prolonged in vast avenues like the radiant prongs of a star. Each of those avenues, planted with tall trees, bore the name of one of the cities of the Confederation and plunged through the ramparts beneath a vault similar to the one that had given access to the young man.

In addition to those broad thoroughfares and the quays of the Iarden, Sodom only offered a tormented tangle of zigzag by-ways, some bending to the irregular forms of buildings, others snaking among the living hedges that enclosed fields and orchards.

On the square, celebratory fires, reduced to incandescent embers, projected intermittent gleams, twisting in capricious undulations the shadows of mutilated statues and pedestals widowed of their teraphim. Naphis' gaze wandered, following the fantastic gestures of those stumps and dancing in the saraband of silhouettes with multiple contortions.

His thought strayed unconsciously over the moving reflections, sinking into the opaque holes with which the side-streets striped the illuminated facades. One of the entrances seemed to be appealing to him; he yielded and penetrated into its obscure sinuosities.

He walked, curiously, alongside the bushes. His gaze plunged into the lush verdure of gardens annexed to palaces whose main entrances opened on to the Avenue of Adama, descending toward the river. Hectic breezes, gliding like gusts of wind over the sea, brushed in with odorous breaths exhaled by the flowering bushes. In the nocturnal peace he perceived stifled echoes, dying chords drawn from kinnors and snatches of drunken song.

From those joyous rumors a poignant cry emerged . . .

Anxiously, he listened . . .

He no longer heard anything but the rustle of the breeze in the moving foliage, the ripple of myrtle-grass under the plash of a stream laughing in the distance as it capered over stones.

A further cry ripped through the darkness: an appeal of terror and despair!

There, facing him, in the depths of a garden, a luminous bay was suddenly cut out in the black wall of a palace. An aerial form sprang forth therefrom, soon followed by the heavy silhouettes of men. Gravel grated, and against the hedge where Naphis was petrified by stupor, a woman with scattered hair and a lacerated veil bloodied her hands in order to fray a passage . . .

The young man extended his arms, seized the fugitive and lifted her up . . . Frightened, she struggled in that unexpected grip; she tried to cry out . . . but the moon surged forth above the somber asphalt walls, the divine rays of which caressed their faces; their contracted lips expanded; they had recognized one another!

Swooning, Maheleth leaned on Naphis' heart.

"Save me!"

"I'm yours."

"Debauchees attacked my litter and abducted me," she explained. "I saw myself dragged to their celebration; I was able to escape, but they pursued me; here they come—defend me."

She took refuge in Naphis' bosom in a spontaneous movement, with the innate loving confidence that makes a chick shelter under the maternal wing. The victor of Hoba enveloped her with a strong arm, while the other placed his menacing hand on the hilt of his sword.

Five men advanced furiously; one of them shouted:

"Man, if you value your life, surrender that woman; she's mine!"

"Who are you to dare to command me?" replied Naphis, proudly.

"That's Noeph, the libertine," murmured Maheleth, whose soft breath brushed her defender's neck like a caress.

"What is it to you? That woman is my slave; I want her!"

Naphis' blade had sprung from its sheath, and the pastor, with a rapid whirl, make it fulgurate in the night.

"You lie!" he roared. "You lie, Noeph the debauchee! This virgin is not and never has been yours, wretch."

"You think so, slave? I've already had the virgin."

"Son of a dog, abject swine. I'll tear out your tongue, as venomous as that of a viper, as perfidious as that of the *maskim*.[1] The day when your mother conceived you, she must have lent her loins to the coupling of unclean spirits; she must have given birth by vomiting . . ."

Noeph bounded under the insult and leapt forward, his sword raised.

Frightened by the sight of weapons, his effeminate companions had fled. His brain troubled by wine fumes, Noeph was lurching heavily.

Naphis' blade whirled and descended; his enemy's weapon, broken at the hilt, left him nothing in his hand but an impotent stump. The impact made him oscillate on his legs; a further impact tipped him over. Naphis bounded upon him, placed his foot on his neck and raised his sword . . .

But a hand retained his arm. Maheleth, hanging on to him, implored him: "Come!"

"Let me nail this scorpion to the ground and free the earth of a malevolent beast," growled the warrior.

---

1 *Maskim* [lirerally, ensnarers] were powerful djinn originating in Akkadian mythology.

"He's no longer to be feared; spare him; let the hour that unites our hands not find them bloody."

"But . . ."

"If you love me!" Maheleth insisted, opening her eyes wide, where her pupils rose in a suppliant flight.

Quivering, Naphis withdrew the foot that weighed upon Noeph's neck, spat on him and drew away, sustaining the woman who was all of his heart.

"This way," she said,

They made their way through the tortuous streets, narrowly linked together. They did not speak, but their hearts understood one another.

Finally, their lips opened, and it was for a kiss . . .

That kiss betrothed them.

Exhausted by the torrential emotions of recent hours, Maheleth felt weak. Naphis sustained her in his muscular arms; she made him a necklace with her own. Slowly, he resumed his march; their mouths no longer quit one another . . .

The blood was flowing in the arteries of the superb male like molten lava; a devouring flame set his body ablaze in the violent blossoming of his virility. He stopped occasionally, ready to collapse on the ground with his burden and annihilate himself in her, but an unusual strength extended his muscles and braced his loins, which were needled by a twinge that was sharp and yet sweet. Everything within him rose to the surface of his being in a pressure that dilated his limbs. Bewildered, he was about to sink into the unknown, the first revelations of which enabled him to glimpse the divinity, when he emerged opposite the temple.

A woman was huddled on the steps, weeping.

The young woman recognized her as her servant Basemath, who was lamenting the abduction of the child and no longer dared present herself before Abimael.

"Basemath!" called Maheleth.

The old nurse raised her head. On perceiving the virgin, white in the lunar light, in the arms of that warrior as handsome as a god, she prostrated herself on the paving stones.

"Praise be to Nergal, the god of war, who has saved the noble virgin; honor to the one whom Nergal has chosen as a spouse."

"Get up, Basemath," Maheleth pronounced. "This is not Nergal but the victor of Hoba; he rescued me from my abductors; he is not a god but he will be a fine husband. This is Naphis, Abram's cherished pastor, and we love one another!"

She extracted herself swiftly from the young man's grasp and disappeared with Basemath into the enclosure of the temple, the postern of which closed heavily.

Stunned, Naphis remained nailed to the spot for some time; but dawn was breaking, palely, in the ether, and the warrior returned to the camp.

V

ABOVE the soft couches of the gynaeceum, amid the heaps of supple fleeces, stripped from Chaldean goats with long silvery hair, a clay lamp suspended from the vault by a triple gold chain projected uneven and tremulous gleams. In the vacillation of shadowed hollows and illuminated planes the undulating contours of two upper bodies in their juvenile bloom were frolicking; then the fleeting lines of the bodies blurred, indecisively, under the flowing creases of fabrics.

Radja and Zogar, Lot's two daughters, were lying next to one another. Only Zogar was asleep; Radja was awake; an unusual gleam enfevered her staring eyes, as if extended toward an image, invisible to all but virtual to her eyes; and the evoked phantom seemed to be attracting her irresistibly . . .

Partly raised on her elbow, Raja measured the jerky somersaults of her unveiled breast, the hardened nipples pointed under the flux and reflux of her oppressed breath like two pink flamingos rocked by the sea and raised by its waves. Her lips were quivering convulsively, crumpling in a bite or blossoming to the appeal of a kiss.

She curled up, knotting her harmonious arms around her half-folded knees, tilting her head over her shoulder with a movement that swelled the neck and the opposed breast in an amorous tension; then her thought, with a rapid evocation, relived the most recent vanished days.

First the terrifying invasion, the engulfment of Sodom by the overflowing tide of the barbarian hordes; the doors of the palace smashed, the appearance of the grim warriors in leather tanned by the sun, with limbs stained with blood, whose powerful silhouettes stood out, livid and sinister, against the red glow of conflagrations. Then the violent, brutal abduction; the fear of the fate reserved for captives; the horror of the contact of those bloody hands on flesh; the audacious gestures that parted the veils; the thick lips parting in lubricious laughter, the bloodshot eyes in which covetousness sparkled.

Then a warrior of tall stature arrived who commanded those men. He contained them with a gesture, traversed their ranks and stopped before the captive virgins.

His avid gaze searched beneath the fabrics, his impatient hand tore them; with his arms, knotted as if the skin were extended over bundles of wet cords, he seized Radja at the base of her back and lifted her up, hollowing it out. She writhed desperately, but the chief threw her into a litter, along with her sister Zogar, and sent them to his tent.

The memory of that grim embrace put another frisson into Radja's back . . . She no longer knew whether it was fear . . .

But then! Prisoners, separated from their father, they departed for the unknown.

A somber departure! Through Sodom in ruins, through the howling rabble of the army gorged with wine, sated of lust, bristling with the spoils of the vanquished . . . A somber departure amid the clamor of triumphant vociferations that insulted their despair; an evil day in which Sodom was gradually seen decreasing on the horizon, and sinking below it forever!

What hope of return could subsist in thought? Whence might deliverance come?

✳

Suddenly, the darkness catches fire; from a luminous nimbus an adolescent emerges, as handsome as Zirbanit, the mother of sensuality,[1] as valiant as Nergal, the champion of the gods. He runs, sweeping away the obstacles, crushing the phalanges and puncturing breasts. His blade flies so rapidly that in the melee it is like lightning, as if the fulgurant zigzags of celestial wrath were slicing through black clouds. One might have thought that his face had detached from the sun all its splendor and light; the enemy collapses before him like palm trees felled by the irresistible blast of the simoom, swallow up in its vortex. Frightened stallions bite one another's breasts, shaking their reins, rear up and break their girth-straps; hooves rattle in their hectic course. The red dew is soon seething in fuming streams, and traces a bloody trail behind them. And the sword is still whirling; its spirals furrows the air with vibrant waves, splashing the ground with ruby fluids, and the warrior approaches the captives' litter, fallen on top of the cadavers of the annihilated escort. Then

---

1 Zirbanit, often rendered Sarpanit, was the consort of the Akkadian god Marduk, primarily associated with the city of Babylon. Her name, meaning "the shining one" probably identified her with the planet Venus, as the present text does, but she was not, strictly speaking, a goddess of amour.

the grim victor parts the leather curtains and his formidable face is transfigured in the radiance of a smile . . . !

The beautiful Radja retained the reflection of that smile in her eyes; by night it floated like a mirage behind her closed eyelids; but today she has seen it again, alive, in broad daylight. Alas, it was no longer flowering for her. She found it again in Naphis' mouth, before the virgin Maheleth!

For that warrior, that demigod, who might have been thought the son of Adar, destroyer of giants, is Naphis, Abram's young pastor, and she loves him!

Already her dream had made a husband of the beloved. No cloud rose over her amorous dawn, no obstacle was raised to bar the route to his heart. Lot would open his daughter's couch joyfully to Abram's favorite, to the warrior who had broken their chains of slavery!

She was living in that hope when Maheleth was revealed to Naphis; the young man gazed at her, and that gaze, sublime with amour, struck Radja directly in the heart.

Heavy tears lurked beneath her eyelids, which closed to real life in order to rediscover the illusion of the dream; they rolled over her cheeks and lips, etching them with bitterness; but her hand wiped them away, energetically. Could she admit defeat without having fought, impotent to triumph?

No! She wanted to hope anyway. She loved him so ardently that she would be able to make herself loved. She fortified herself in that assurance, took pleasure in the spectacle of her beauty, counted on her charms to conquer the man she wanted to be her master, sensing him already hers, and her moist lips stammered, in an invasive intoxication:

"Naphis! My Naphis!"

The words caught in her throat . . .

Two eyes blazed in the penumbra, burning hers. Zogar had raised herself up; she leaned toward Radja and hissed, her teeth grating and her voice hoarse:

"What did you say? Repeat it . . . ! Oh, shut up . . . Naphis, your Naphis! Fool, you shall not have him, you shall not take him from me; he's mine; I want him for myself, for myself alone!"

"For yourself?" exclaimed Radja, pushing her sister away with an abrupt gesture and straightening herself with a nervous twitch. "Fool yourself— he doesn't love you and never will."

She was naked, superb and triumphant, drowned in the coppery waves of her rutilant tresses, which spilled over the splendor of her shoulders, undulated, running over the arched line of her back, and then rebounded at its base in a further fall, all the way to the feet emerging from the silvery waves that uplifted the Chaldean furs; it splashed their heels and roseate soles with a phosphorescent foam, while in her face, over the ivory of the rounded declivities of the flesh, a wild gleam lit up, like the radiance emanated by a hearth of amour.

"Why shouldn't he love me?" replied Zogar. "I'm beautiful; I have skin as soft as the flesh of a lily and the down of a swan; my lips are rich with warm blood, my opulent breasts will make a soft pillow for his head. He will collect my *bethoulim* in an intoxication that will overwhelm, in him, all known sensualities.

"Dare you talk about your virginity? Although no man has possessed you, your senses have already yielded under the refined caresses of your slaves. You have enervated yourself in solitary pleasures, and too often, the lambskins of your couch have drunk the dew of your enjoyments!"

"Are you without sin, then, to reproach me? Have you never sought the sensuality that haunts your dreams? Have you not deceived the ardors of your puberty by demanding from your sexual parts the male pleasures that you lack, the obsession of which exacerbates your senses?"

"Never, you hear, never!" cried Radja, exasperated by the incredulous rictus that tucked up

Zogar's lips. "I'm worthy of the love of Naphis. He's pure. You're not made for him."

"Pure, you say? Do you not know that new natures are the easiest to conquer, for savant lovers? I shall be able to take possession of him, envelop him with my odor, excite his desires, guide them, exasperate them with my passion and, if necessary, by his own resources . . ."

She laughed, revealing her sharp teeth, inflating her bloody lips, flaring her nostrils dilated by eroticism.

Her hand was buried in the fabrics; suddenly, her teeth clicked, her breast heaved, her eyes revulsed and were extinguished, and she fell back in a spasm . . .

Radja sniggered. The disdainful creases that compressed the corners of her mouth were gradually effaced; only a vertical furrow hollowed out in her forehead brought her eyebrows closer together, arching their curvature. A violent labor was engendered in her thought. Then her physiognomy was united in an impassive mask, as impenetrable as the surface of a dormant pool.

She looked at her sister. Zogar emerged from her prostration. Then she spoke:

"For the moment, our quarrels are sterile and dangerous. It isn't one of us that Naphis loves. Let's unite our forces against the one who is taking him from us. After the victory, we can settle the matter together."

"Another?" roared Zogar. "Name her!"

"The daughter of Abimael, Maheleth, our companion."

"How can he love her? How could he have met her?"

"You can't see, Zogar. I've observed and I've seen. When Bara and her father offered her to Abram, Naphis was beside our uncle. Their gazes met and I saw a mutual amour born in their eyes."

"By Ninge the infernal goddess, she shall die!"[1]

"The daughter of the Great Cohen?"

"She shall die, I tell you, if Naphis loves her, or I shall die.!"

"Don't excite yourself thus," said Radja, constraining her sister to sit down beside her; "you don't know that our father has asked Abram, and obtained his consent, to retain our liberator in the palace for a few days. Tomorrow, Naphis will be our guest. Undoubtedly our parents are dreaming of an alliance between him and one of us. I'm the elder; well, I'll abandon the prerogatives of my

---

1 Ninge is an Akkadian version of the name of the consort of Bel, transformed in the Old Testament as Baal.

rank, for if we compete with one another we might both lose him, to the profit of Maheleth. Listen, I'm not jealous; let him belong to both of us!"

Zogar lowered her head pensively.

"In any case," Radja insinuated, "I might be mistaken about the power of his love for Abimael's daughter. You can see, therefore, that I'm being generous in offering to share him with you, when I could have him to myself, by right of being older. Nevertheless, I think the seed of his passion for Maheleth is dangerous. It's necessary to destroy it without delay, before it has put down ineradicable roots. It's necessary to envelop Naphis in unfamiliar sensualities, ever renascent, and, in order to efface in him the dream-vision of a virgin, to give him the living possession of two women. It's necessary that our kisses furrow his body so narrowly that there will be no place thereon that has not been ours, that does not bear the imprint of our lips and our caresses."

"So be it," said Zogar, overwhelmed by her sister's imperious speech.

"Tomorrow, we'll go to bathe in the Iarden with the noble daughters of Sodom. Maheleth will be there. Let's spy on her."

VI

MAHELETH and her companions emerged from Sodom at first light. In the Orient, the veils of night were tearing and floating in the ether, detaching their somber draperies from the brightening horizon. The silhouettes of palm trees loomed up black and motionless; clumps of lemon-trees were agglomerated in confused and inert masses. No breath of wind troubled the calm and silence of nature, still dormant. In the great meditation, only the sound of myrtle-grass, vibrant under the kiss of the water, exhaled its muted musical murmur on the grassy bank of the river.

In the distance the hills rose up, profiling their neatly circled crests, their bases drowned in a dense mist that was degraded half way up, no longer leaving anything but threads of gray vapor trailing along escarpments or surrounding the white heads of the highest peaks with smoky crowns.

Gradually, the Orient turned crimson; the shreds of the clouds, swept by the dawn, fringed by luminous hems and striped with bloody splashes, soon melted away in the radiation of the sun, which was still imperceptible. The earth awoke, opened its eyes and respired.

A light breeze ran over the countryside, extracting it from its torpor; the rustling crops undulated in blond waves from which ruby, sapphire and amethyst gleams emerged in places, poppies, cornflowers and rye-grass enameling the gilded fleece of the ripe wheat. Olive groves scattered their flowers in the air and carpeted the ground with a creamy powder; palm trees swayed their feathery crests above orange-groves and oleanders, whose powerful effluvia charged the atmosphere with heady aromas.

Finally, the sun appeared in all its glory. The mountains, previously blue, caught alight in the general blaze; the masses of shadow crouching at the feet of the trees made the bright colors of flowers and foliage stand out more; the waters of the Iarden shone like the facets of a diamond, blinding the eyes with their moving reflections.

And everywhere, from all the nests, all the fallow land and all the branches, rose the hum of insects, the song of cicadas and the universal chirping of birds. A skylark rose up toward the zenith with a flutter of wings, dispersing its hectic trills, carrying to God the hymn of the love of living nature . . .

The virgins undressed in the slender shade of tamarisks and the protective shelter of myrtle-grass, whose thick curtain defied indiscreet gazes. The freshness of the morning unfurled in light waves over their chilly nudity, adding a sheen to the amber-tinted ivory of their juvenile flesh. Then they plunged into the waves, still lukewarm in spite of the nocturnal dew. Their milky bodies combined harmoniously with the flowering water-lilies; joyful cries mingled with the pearly laughter and the exclamations of timid late arrivals hesitating on the bank and testing the water with their feet.

Maheleth was swimming vigorously; her arms cleaved the current with a bold thrust, rounded out in gracious curves, to depart again with a new surge. The broken water seethed around the virgin's flanks, festooning her with a girdle of foam. The wake threaded a babbling splash behind her feet and faded away in the course of the river, constellated with bubbles of air that evaporated immediately.

Maheleth came ashore on an islet and sat down on the mossy hyssop that carpeted its edge. Her loose hair collapsed in loose swathes, cloaking her rounded shoulders and her arched back. One hank snaked over her neck, swept her throat and settled in the narrow cleft between her breasts. Oppressed by the exercise of swimming, they swelled and collapsed with a precipitate rhythm; Maheleth's curt breath caused their whiteness to stand out in all its purity and the azure network of veins in which blood was flowing was outlined against the mat skin.

Meanwhile, the radiant sun continued its ascensional progress; the firmament was displayed, purified of all cloud, fluttering with luminous waves that dappled its azure. Heat floated over the landscape, rendered more intense by the reverberation of the water and the overheated soil.

Regretfully, Maheleth and her companions emerged from the water in order to return to the city in the protective shade of the great avenue of sycamores.

Naphis was indulging in the enjoyments of bathing when the daughters of Sodom arrived. He hid on the islet and soon saw their frolics begin. He strove to discover his beloved on the beach, amid the whiteness of the foam raised by the tangle of burnished flesh. While his gaze was attached to the groups that were timidly paddling near the edge a splash of cleaved water caught his ear; at the same time the crumpled reeds opened and closed alongside the bush in which he was hidden, and Maheleth came ashore on the islet.

Anxious, suppressing the heaving of his breast, Naphis was prey to tumultuous emotions. He wanted to fill his eyes with the beauties of the woman he loved. Only the gnarled trunk of a tamarisk and a thin curtain of furze hid her from his gaze. He glimpsed her pert foot stirring the water and launching it in a spray whose droplets were iridescent in the sunlight. Her breath reached him through the crystalline patter of the water's kisses vibrating on the pebbles and licking the mosses.

He would have liked to draw closer to her, but the stems creaked under the pressure of his body and the fear of betraying his presence immobilized him immediately. His thought penetrated the obstacle, however, whipping his desire and irritating its progressive acuity; he was about to cede to it when the water splashed him with its spray. Maheleth returned to the bank.

He glimpsed the pink tones of fleeing lines momentarily in the semitransparency of the troubled waves, and then they were veiled by the mantle of floating hair rolling on the surface of the river in the virgin's wake, like blonde clouds emerging from the green-tinted current; finally, everything disappeared behind the sinuosities of the islet.

Immediately, Naphis let himself slide silently into the water, and reached the shore at a neighboring bend. From there he went back up the course of the river, hiding in the myrtle-grass, and purloined Maheleth's necklace, in order to bring the young woman back to the bank of the Iarden alone in search of her jewel.

The troop of young women drew away, laughing nonchalantly; gradually, the sound of their voices faded and their silhouettes were lost in the verdant avenue. Lying in the myrtle-grass, Naphis raised himself up on his elbow and watched the path along which Maheleth had disappeared, impatiently . . .

Eventually, he sees her coming back, at a run, to the place where the droplets that had caressed her flesh seem to be weeping their lost sensuality over the moist grass. The sprigs shiver at the murmur of her speech and stir at the contact of her fingers, which part them, searching for the lost jewel. And the grass wonders how, for an adornment of human manufacture, the virgin could scorn the liquid pearls that have kissed her beauty. Hyssop has perfumed them with its aroma, the sun has made them iridescent with its rays, but Maheleth disperses them disdainfully with her searching hand. Kneeling on the moss, supporting herself with one arm on the ground, she extends her flexible neck, and that pose develops the elegant undulations of her body. Nothing is hidden beneath the young growth. Then her gaze interrogates the water of the river, which is flowing transparently over the sparkling sand of the bank. She only sees her own image there, and the smile of the waves at her beauty brings a smile to her lips. Her thought wanders and, as if responding to her dream, another image comes to unite with her own. A breath brushing the moss stirs the nape of her neck, a kiss makes her straighten up, intoxicated and quivering . . .

Naphis is beside her!

Alarmed by his own audacity, but simultaneously intoxicated by the savor that his lips have retained, the young man is nonplussed and dares not look at the young woman whose modesty has caused her also to lower her eyes. But soon their foreheads are raised together, illuminated by such a radiance that an immense joy fills the heart of Naphis and exalts his ardor. His hands grip the arms that are hanging limply along Maheleth's body and draw the young woman toward him. She yields, unconsciously, to the charm that summons her, and in order to hide her blush, presses her head against her beloved's breast.

For an instant they remain united, souls overflowing with an inexpressible emotion, engulfed in the eruption of their amour. Then Naphis, impatient in his desire, kneels at Maheleth's feet and forces her lowered eyes to repose on his own; he stares at them with so much surging passion that they seem to the virgin to be brushing her eyes with a kiss. She smiles at him, and Naphis allows ardent words to flow from his heart,

"How beautiful you are, my beloved! Who, among all women, could compete with you in splendor? The most superb would pale at your aspect, as the moon is extinguished in the firmament when the sun lights up. Your hair undulates like clusters of laburnum, like wheat yellowing in the evening breeze; cinnamon embalms it and speckles it like the morning dew dripping over the crops. Your complexion seems to be made of a single lily petal over which roses of Sharon are blooming. Your eyes sparkle with golden reflections of chrysolith, their lashes curl and spread the aromas of the hyssop that grows on the banks of the Iarden. Your lips have the brightness of pomegranates in flower and the savor of its fruits, and your teeth are as nacreous as marine pearls. The dimples of your cheeks blossom under your smile like the rosy corollas of a peach-tree under the caress of spring zephyrs. Your chin has the graceful curve of a dove's wing, your neck the suave inflexions of a swan's, and its delicate creases are reminiscent of little streams lost in a meadow. Mountain goats would envy the slenderness of your arched feet; your hands are ivory encrusted with the pearls of your polished fingernails . . .

"Remove, O elect of my soul, the veil that hides your other beauties from my gaze; allow yourself to be contemplated in your splendor; let your reality dazzle my eyes with the radiation of treasures that surpass everything my thought has been able to dream . . ."

As the firmament darkens, while retaining a rutilant glow in the occident, when the sun descends below the horizon, so Maheleth's face was veiled, turning crimson with modesty, when her eyelids descended over her troubled pupils in response to those words. Naphis' voice went straight to her heart, and her breasts quivered like two twins in their mother's womb. The virgin did not think of fleeing; the pastor's words were as sweet to her the milk of the goats that graze the odorous herbs of Mount Sanir. Naphis' breath exhaled the myrrh with which he had embalmed his mouth and ran over Maheleth's pink face, causing her flared nostrils to palpitate voluptuously.

Naphis went on:

"Let me remove this veil, which I shall spread over our heads like a flag of glory, like a summer sky swarming with stars! Then, O my beauty, you will no longer have anything hidden from the spouse of your soul, and I will reveal amour to you! Yield to the imperious desire that is swelling your bosom; slake my thirst with delicious wine from the spring of your nipples, and I will pour out the intoxicating liquor in long floods; I will enable you to share the intoxication that inundates sensuality!"

Boldly, his hand unfastened the clasp of Maheleth's veil; with a modest movement she retained him with two hands over her breasts, while her elbows tightened against her body in a fearful attitude.

Naphis enlaces the virgin's flexible waist, which flexes like a young palm tree under a storm-wind. Already, his avid lips have brushed the beloved's, whose panting breath causes the pastor's curly down to undulate; he is about to tip her back on the moss when, as supple as a gazelle, she slips from his embrace and flees.

Surprised at first, he is soon on her heels, and catches up with her in a clump of oleanders, kneeling on the edge of a spring, bathing her burning head. He leans over, his arms open . . .

But she gazes at him with the suppliant mildness of a wounded turtle-dove, and he stops, vanquished.

VII

WHEN Maheleth abandoned her companions in order to go back down the Iarden, Radja and her sister exchanged a glance in which the same suspicion gleamed. Gradually, they slowed their pace, allowing the chattering cortege of young women to file before them, which was already disbanding, spreading out along the path in enlaced couples or laughing groups. Radja knelt down beside a clump of mandrakes, summoned her sister to help her pick them, and sent her in quest of a flexible shoot with which to tie the bundle.

But she has turned her head; her gaze has ranged over the surrounding area and she has seen that she is quite alone. As supple as a panther, with one bound, she rejoins Zogar in a wood, the gentle declivity of which slopes all the way to the river bank. They glide from tree to tree, drawing closer, muffling their footfalls and holding their breath. Suddenly, they halt. Maheleth is there, before their eyes, pliant in Naphis' embrace . . .

They cannot hear the lovers' words, but passion shines in their faces. Then the daughter of Abimael slips away and flees, coming to seek shelter in the clump of oleanders that confines their hiding-place.

Lot's daughters have soon gone on ahead again, and they reenter Sodom, preceding Maheleth by some distance, who follows the avenue of sycamores at a slow pace. Her heart is beating like the loins of a mother where a conceived child is waking to life; her breast is panting ardently, as if in the keen air of a rapid run. The blood turning her cheeks crimson puts a fire behind her eyelids. Her moist eyes allow their errant gaze to wander over the landscape and return to stare at the ground with a fearful confusion. However, she feels happy, experiencing the joy of living, for life is good for her. The exhaustion of her body, bruised by emotions, allows her soul to bound lightly, as if two Kherubim were carrying it away on their wings in their irresistible flight. She is happy; she is in love and is beloved!

Naphis! Her handsome Naphis! She murmurs that name in a low voice, which, in flowing from her lips distils the sweetness of a honeycomb and the perfumed taste of a ripe apple. She is intoxicated by the kiss that was placed on her lips and which her mouth is still breathing in. She, who trembled before the severe Abram, the patriarch whose bed she was to share, as a resigned victim, is flying today toward the fiancé of her heart in a great surge of amour!

Love, virgin of Sodom, amour is smiling on your youth; love, your heart is swelling like a bud into which the sap of spring is rising; the sun is pouring its radiance over you, the flowers are intoxicating you with their amorous exhalations, the seductive breezes are brushing you with their kisses and, playing amid your floating curls, and gliding over your quivering flesh, their caress is ever more gentle, ever more forceful . . . Love! The bud is opening, the lily blossoming, the beloved is about to settle in its bosom . . . . . .

Still lost in her dream, Maheleth traverses the arched square on to which the door giving access to the temple gardens opens, without seeing two furtive silhouettes turn away from her path. She arrives at the building and goes up to the high priest's apartments. She goes in, and with a habitual movement, comes to offer her forehead to her father's kiss.

Abimael pushes her away and, holding her under his inquisitive gaze, speaks to her in an irritated voice:

"Where are you coming from so late?"

Maheleth is troubled; her youth has not yet learned to lie; but immediately, the valor of her amour substitutes for the inexperience of her candor; she raises her eyelids, momentarily lowered, and, covering her father with a limpid gaze, she replies seductively:

"Aren't you going to kiss your daughter, Father?"

With an adorable thrust of the arms she imprisons the Cohen's neck; standing up on the toes of her sandals, she holds his head and places her youthful lips on Abimael's snowy beard.

But the latter throws his head back, breaks the caressant necklace enlacing him with a brutal gesture and repeats:

"Where are you coming from?"

"But . . . from bathing!" said the young woman, with an ingenuous astonishment.

"Your companions returned a long time ago."

"Oh, that's it!" she said, shaking her head as if to explain her stupidity. "At the gates of the city I had to go back down the Iarden. When I got dressed I forgot my necklace in the grass of the river bank . . . you know, my beautiful necklace of chrysoliths . . . the one you brought me back from the land of Mizraim. It was so hot," she added, stretching lazily, "that I would have hesitated to remake such a long journey, and I would have abandoned it if I didn't value it so highly . . . but it's precious to me since it came from you."

While chattering, the ingenious debauchee had taken possession of the paternal forehead again, furrowing it with kisses while her agile hands smoothed Abimael's beard coquettishly.

The Great Cohen maintained his severe physiognomy.

"You didn't meet anyone?"

"Who do you expect me to have met . . . ?" Maheleth commenced. But she saw a menacing crease hollow out between her father's frowning eyebrows; she guessed that someone had been spying on her, that she had been betrayed; she did not lose her courage and continued, after slapping her forehead: "How foolish I am! Yes, I encountered one of the pastors of that Abram who did not want me for a wife."

"What did you say?"

"Nothing at first. Then, seeing me searching the grass, he asked me what I was looking for. 'This,' I replied, as I had just found my necklace. He offered to accompany me to the city. I thanked him and I added that I had no need of anyone."

"Who is this pastor?"

"I searched momentarily; his features were not unknown to me. It seemed to me, however, that it was the young man who was standing to the right of the Hebrew when the troops returned—but I would not dare affirm it."

"You're lying!"

"Father!"

"You're lying, I tell you! You know his name and I can confound you. It's Naphis, Abram's favorite; you know him. He talked to you amorously!"

Disconcerted, Maheleth lowered her eyes and bowed her head. In the heavy silence of the apartment the light susurrus of the sand-glass slowly measured the minutes; the thin thread swelled the inferior cone; the last grains slid through . . . Only then did the beating of the virginal heart precipitate its staccato echoes.

Motionless, his mouth rigid, Abimael remained silent.

That frightful silence oppressed Maheleth; she assembled all her courage and threw herself at the Great Cohen's knees.

"You're right; forgive me . . . I lied. Yes, it was Naphis."

"I knew that."

Those words fell lugubriously; a frisson of alarm shook the virgin's shoulders; she stiffened, still hoping to vanquish.

"It was Naphis! He loves me and I love him!"

"Wretch!" growled Abimael, his hands raised as if for an anathema.

"Oh, you don't understand, Father! I hid it from you in order to spare you a dolor and a just anger. Listen: on the evening of the fête held in honor of the deliverance of Sodom, while you were attending the feast with King Bara, I was returning to the lodgings in my litter. Still confused by my presentation to the Hebrew, I wasn't paying any heed to the route I was following. Suddenly, an eddy in the crowd separated my nurse Basemath from the cortege. Then I heard cries and my porters began to run. Before I had recovered from my amazement, I heard a door slam; I parted the curtains; I was in an unfamiliar place. I tried to cry out but I was carried off; I struggled, but I was imprisoned. My slaves, bribed, had sold me. Night fell; I was dragged into the midst of debauchees who, already drunk, tried to put their hands on me. I was able to open a window, jump through it and run to the hedge; I tried to force a way through it, impotently, and my abductors were on my heels. Alone in the night, I was doomed! Naphis happened to be there. He defied the wretches, helped me and saved me; then he escorted me to the temple. I owe my virginity to him. This morning, he told me that he loved me; my heart knew that already . . ."

She had straightened up, reassured, strengthened by the amour exalted by her confession; she supported herself upon it as on an unbreakable pedestal; she adorned herself with it like a glory.

Abimael had listened to her without a single crease in his face relaxing; when she finished, he pronounced:

"No matter! You will never belong to that man."

"Father!"

"Daughter devoid of pride! You did not feel, then, the insult made to our blood by the Hebrew? You dare to love a man of that race?"

"Naphis is not of Abram's family. He was born in Gamora."

"He is the Hebrew's favorite, and my hatred envelops everything that belongs to him. In any case, I have already chosen your husband. Prepare to be the wife of Noeph."

"Noeph! Oh, my Lord," cried Maheleth, "he is the one who tried to profane me; he was my cowardly abductor . . ."

"I know that; he confessed it to me, as well as his long-standing love for you," the Cohen lied. "Passion is his excuse; I forgave him, and I am giving you to him."

"Father, Father, listen to me, you haven't heard me," the unfortunate child begged through her sobs, her eyes bulging with horror, wringing her hands, her arms raised in a supreme invocation. "He wanted, after having soiled me, to deliver me to the appetites of all his companions. Father, if you love me, save me from that man!"

Noeph was cherished by the Great Cohen. His effeminate body, saturated by perfumes, had tempted Abimael's lust; ambitious, the debauchee had thought of exploiting the old man's passion and setting his union with Mahaleth as the price of his complaisance—not because he loved the virgin, but because of the elevated situation that a relationship with the priest of Nabou would give him. The Cohen, in his rancor against Abram, who scorned his gods, was throwing his daughter to that abject marriage. The amour of the elected son of the Hebrew for Mahaleth ought to have effaced the recent grievance of the sudden refusal, but at that moment, his desire for Noeph, stimulating his appetites, ignited his hatred.

He therefore went on: "Return to the gynaeceum. You will only quit it for Noeph's abode. I have spoken."

He pushed away the unfortunate young woman who was kissing his knees and clinging to the hem of his robe; then he clapped his hands twice. Maheleth's women and eunuchs came running. He gave them an order to take her to her apartments and prohibit all communication with the exterior.

Standing up, implacable, he watched her leave. Annihilated by the terrible depth of her fall, collapsed with the ruins of the happiness glimpsed and already condemned, she abandoned herself to Basemath's arms; her flexible waist undulated in a suave harmony of lines, of which chaste youth did not allow the voluptuous forms to be revealed. Her head, borne by the excessive weight of her scattered hair, tipped neck, and the silky waves, sweeping the paving-stones, unfurled a golden wake behind her. With a familiar gesture, Abimael lifted his bushy beard over his mouth in order to dissimulate a hideous smile

He was thinking about Noeph . . .

His thoughts wandered, creating strange couplings, lubricious contortions and infamous postures. He grouped, in one unique and multiple vision, the abominations of his lust. His trembling hand wandered in empty space, seeking the contact of his obscene evocations; titillations tickled his enervated loins, imprinting a renascent vigor therein. He sniggered as he imagined the imminent wedding: the man polluted by him in his daughter's nuptial bed . . . and the image of the soiled and violated virgin melted into an enlacement of swarming flesh . . .

His daughter! And his mouth was drooling . . . !

From the threshold of the apartment, Maheleth cast a supreme appeal to her father. He looked at her . . . and following his frightful dream, no longer had any consciousness of his paternity. In her despair, that woman had contortions of dolor that caused him to evoke the spasmodic clench. He was enraged by the semi-treasons of the fabrics that plastered her body, and soon undressed her with his eyes. From then on, one single thought haunted him: the thought of that young flesh, alive, kneaded by amour; his incestuous gaze clung to the erect summits of the breasts, which cleaved the taut cloth, slid over the torso, hesitated at the hips, and then plunged all the way to the arcane mystery in which the immaculate rose flourished. His eyes blazed . . .

He did not reply, no longer hearing; but he contemplated her, panting. When the door closed again behind her he leaned forward as if drawn in her wake by an invincible fascination. He extended his arms, opened his mouth . . . and then collapsed on the cushions, murmuring:

"She's very beautiful!"

VIII

NAPHIS has rapped with his staff on the threshold of Lot's palace. He is coming as Abram's son. Immediately, two young black slaves brought back from the land of Khoush have taken off his garments and conducted him to the porphyry bath where the perfumed and soothing warmth of limpid water is awaiting him. Then they rub the foreigner's body with fine linen cloths, anointing his limbs with aromatics, after having made the joints supple by means of the massage of their skillful hands. They comb the curls of his hair, lustrous with cinnamon, and rub his feet with mesdjem. Then he is dressed again in a light tunic and a sumptuous robe, the scarlet wool of which is sown with zircons. Sandals, each fabricated with a thin lath of olive-wood circled with silver, are attached to his ankles by supple leather straps made from the skin of goat-kids.

On his head a crown is placed in which the redness of pomegranate flowers burst forth amid the somber verdure of laurels.

The victor of Hoba advances, guided by the black slaves. The son of Harran comes to meet him and places his hands on his shoulders as a pledge of welcome. Behind Lot stand his wife and his daughters; they are carrying matzo, fruits, milk and wine harvested from the renowned hills of Shiloh.

The Hebrew invites Lot to lie down next to him on cushions covered in the fur of Oriental goats, the silky hair of which has been plunged twice into Phoenician crimson. The Master's wife presents unleavened bread; Lot takes it and extends it to Naphis, who breaks it with him.

The servants place an entire lamb before the guests, roasted over a hot fire, the golden skin of which rises up in crusty blisters. Radja, standing next to the chief of Abram's pastors, fills the cups again as soon as the men have emptied them. Zogar, sitting on her heels, makes the strings of a kinnor vibrate. Cassolettes fume, exhaling aromas of amber and incense. Wines, dishes, songs and perfumes, everything is intoxication and sensuality.

Then pink watermelons with black pips were served, the melting pulp of which refreshed lips irritated by the seasoning and spices of the meat and the fire of fermented grapes. Then there were juicy figs, fat cheeses, honey cakes kneaded with fine wheat flour, cooked over red-hot stones and sprinkled with cumin. Finally, in woven wicker baskets, there were pyramids of fruits: scented apples, ripe pomegranates laughing through the cracks in their peel, grapes streaming with red and gold tears, oranges with tones as warm as the cheeks of the beautiful daughters of Chaldea; bunches of dates, lemons and limes heaped on thuya platters. In large red earthenware pots, broths of wheat and barley fumed, acacia flowers floated on yellow camel-milk, which they impregnated with their perfume, in alabaster jars.

A swollen gourd of lotus wine from the land of Mizraim was brought. Radja filled a vessel with it and inclined it over her arm. As she poured it for the guest she raised her elbow in such a way as to show the down of her armpit, emitting voluptuous emanations of its intoxicating odor in gusts. At the same time, she made her breasts stand out, leaning over far enough to brush the young man's cheek and caress his forehead with her ardent breath, saturated with myrrh, breathing her desire; beneath her eyelids, lowered in a feline fashion. Her gaze filtered a radiance through her lashes, provoking the guest's. She pressed his hip with her knee as she bent it in order to serve him; her round bare arm rested on his shoulder and slid over his inclined neck.

The meal finished. Radja lay down among the fleeces and tipped her upper body back in a weary attitude that belied the undulation of her lascivious hips. Between her slightly parted lips her sharp teeth laughed, inviting kisses, and even bites.

And Naphis saw nothing!

In vain the feet flutter on the paving stones, marking out a concentrated impatience; in vain the tunic gapes over the cleavage of the breasts as the arms stretch, which then exaggerate the pose by folding back behind the nape of the neck; in vain the eyes fulgurate their burning passion; the young man remains impassive . . . Another image fills his eyes; another evocation is resplendent in his heart . . .

The torrid heat becomes heavy. Radja gets up. She picks up a large leaf of a date-palm and agitates it above Naphis' moist forehead. She uses that fan as a screen to hide from anyone else the teasing winks with which she peppers the handsome pastor. With a lazy and enervated movement she drops the leaf and, bending down to pick it up, her lips brush the nape of the adolescent, who shudders . . .

Radja had a triumphant gleam in her eyes.

Naphis tilted his head back and smiled at her, but on seeing her he passed his hand over his forehead with a disillusioned gesture, as if awakening from the sweetness of a beautiful dream . . . The kiss that he had received did not respond to the one evoked by his dream!

Lot was drowsy. In his turn, Naphis yielded to somnolence. Radja resumed agitating her fan in order to protect the sleeper's face from mosquitoes. Gradually, she leaned over, bent her knees, let herself fall beside him, supported herself on her elbow momentarily, and moved her head hesitantly toward the pastor's.

Naphis was profoundly asleep, his lips parted; droplets of sweat were pearling on his temples; the young woman wiped them away gently. He did not budge. Then she became bolder, lay down on the mat, and her feline body flowed against that of the coveted man . . .

That contact did not wake Naphis, but gave substance to his dreams. He opened his arms. The amorous woman, excited, insinuated herself into their grasp. Through the supple cloth she felt the male flesh panting, his loins vibrating with desire. She adhered to him more tightly, wrapping her seductive legs around the thighs of the sleeper and shoving her hungry belly against the rigid blossoming of his virility . . . her mouth drank the kiss floating on his lips, and as she fell backwards, rushing his loins more forcefully toward the ultimate caress, in the paroxysm of appetite into which the stolen kiss threw her, a murmur came to strike her directly in the heart . . .

"Maheleth!" stammered Naphis.

That name! Always that phantom between her and him.

And, facing her, Zogar was sniggering!

Humiliated and furious, she pulled away, distancing herself angrily from the Gamoran, crumpling between her clenched fingers the fan that she was still holding.

And water, trickling in droplets into a basin, wept, echoing the tears that, in the distant gynaeceum, were streaming over the streaked cheeks of Maheleth, captive in the prison that was the tomb of her amour. She was weeping, mad with dolor, not knowing that those who had betrayed her were, at that moment, seeking to steal her lover from her, after having stolen her liberty.

In her despair, in the darkness that shrouded her life, Maheleth, in spite of everything, wanted to see again, like a faintly twinkling star, an inviolable radiance, the glimmer of imperishable amour!

Weep, virgin of Sodom, weep, slave sold to lust, the salary of your father's debauchery!

✳

But Naphis wakes up . . . His eyes, opening, wander in search of the Beloved who populated his dream . . . His thought hesitates in the presence of the novel frame that surrounds him . . . Gradually, it frees itself from its clouds; the last fog evaporates . . .

He remembers. He is the guest of the son of Harran. The patriarch is there, sitting before him; he has emerged from his torpor and is covering him with a paternal smile. His two daughters are dissimulating the expression of their faces in the shadow of an enormous stele at the base of which they are crouching. They seem indifferent, abandoned to the nonchalance of the hot hours . . . and in spite of the evidence, Naphis can only believe that the visions of his slumber and the sensations experienced were absolute chimeras. His hallucination had palpable forms, his grasp cannot have encircled emptiness, the collected kiss was alive! But no! He has only lived that moment next to a phantom, and the conviction of his deceptive felicity leaves a heaviness in his brain, putting a bitterness on his lips.

A clear voice springs forth in the silence, shelling out its pearly notes like the scattering of the jet of water pulverized in the onyx shell; Zogar speaks to the Patriarch.

"Father and Lord, you doubtless know the news from the city?"

"No," replies the Hebrew. "Announce it to us, my child, and let the good news spill from your mouth."

"The rich Noeph, the son of Hetheus the Hethean, is taking the daughter of Abimael in marriage."

"Maheleth!"

"Yes," Zogar affirmed. "The Great Cohen of Nabou was wounded by our uncle's refusal; he has not wanted his daughter to bear the insult for long. Noeph solicited her alliance, Abimael agreed to it. The betrothal is concluded and the marriage imminent, Maheleth made us the confidence of it while bathing this morning."

"May Elohim spread his benedictions over them!" exclaimed the patriarch, lifting his hands in a broad gesture of protection and prayer. "Maheleth is gentle, beautiful and pure. Next to her, Noeph will forget his former debauchery; I hope so and believe so. His amour will no longer go to anyone but her once she has slept on his bosom. She merits being a happy wife, as she has been a noble daughter."

Naphis had not uttered a cry or a word. His two torturers, however, were watching his face. He went pale; sweat was oozing from his livid temples; his discolored lips were trembling convulsively.

The howl that despair was about to extract from him had been stopped in his contracted throat. He was suffocated by it and his pallor was now streaked with violet patches. Finally, he exhaled a hoarse sigh.

He was clawed by a terrible anguish. Maheleth! What, that very morning she had delivered her lips to his kiss and confirmed by all the manifestations of her being the shared amour born under the ramparts of Sodom and confessed on the night of her deliverance, and all that while she was the fiancée of another?

And what other? The infamous abductor from whom he, Naphis, had saved her! It was impossible! He did not believe it; he did not want to believe it . . . and yet? Why had she made him spare that Noeph, whom she ought to have hated, when he held him under his avenging arm? Besides which, the news, brutally announced, must be veridical; what motive could have dictated a lie to his host's daughters, the companions of his beloved?

He still doubted, in spite of the evidence. His reason had to yield to the intuition of his heart . . .

Oh, he could not live in that anxiety . . . he had to know . . .

How? What did it matter? He would know, because he wanted to know!

IX

WHEN slumber had extended its somber span over the guests of the palace and touched their heavy eyelids with its wing; when only the even respiration of the young women, the powerful breathing of the patriarch and the hoarse snores of the slaves exhausted by the day's labor betrayed the life latent beneath the lethargy of the dwelling, Naphis got up from his couch.

Maheleth was summoning him! His heart beating rapidly, instinctively, he listened, without thinking that the voice heard might only be the echo of the obsessive thought to which he had succumbed. After the prostration of the day, his brain awoke, populated by hallucinations so clear that he believed himself to be lucid.

He still extended his ear, the blood that was seething within him, hammering his temples, filled it with a strange buzz in which the mysterious whispers of the night were confounded: the woodwork that was creaking as if exhaling a gasp; the dull beating of the padded wings of owls; the soft frictions of heir tenebrous amours . . .

But he is not mistaken! A sigh . . . a name . . . Naphis!

Stifling his footfalls, he glides along the corridors, unlatches the door, crosses the threshold and runs toward the heard appeal . . . toward Maheleth.

And yet, in the dwelling that he abandoned, the name of Naphis renewed and prolonged its echoes, exhaled by a double dream. But how far the pastor was from the thought that was haunting the dreams of Radja and Zogar, of which it was the phantom.

Amorous fools, your secret wandered over your lips, escaped from the depths of your being; like a bird whose aviary is opened, it has taken flight and is preparing tears for you. The whisper of your desires has awakened another, and the man that your arms wanted to retain has departed, at your invitation, toward the amour that is rendering you desperate!

Night had reached the middle of its course; the lights of the city were going out one by one; a few fires, lit in the open air, were dying, emitting intermittent gleams, like eyes heavy with slumber blinking before closing. Appeasement numbed the city, previously noisy and lascivious. Sometimes, the rapid click of the sandals of some belated pedestrian rang out, soon to fade away. From distant palaces a few notes of a drinking song emerged faintly, dispersed by the warm gusts of seductive breezes. Mysterious sobs evoked debaucheries sheltered behind the unfathomable walls of those repairs of abomination. Under the somber arcades of a portico, a filthy group agitated confusedly, its members delivering themselves to obscene lusts.

The firmament was a pure deep blue, over which radiant stars were dotted, deploying in all its amplitude the royal sash of its nebulous swarm of stars; the diamante flood scintillated in the azure like the pulverized water a cascade filtering solar rays. Their diffuse light disaggregated the darkness, a mystical reflection of the invisible and all-seeing gaze of the Almighty. A balsamic breeze, poured forth by the mountains, swept away the impure exhalations of the day. Over the somnolent city floated the effluvia of orange trees in flower; great lilies exhaled their perfumed soul; myrtle-grass rattled, swayed by the wind; all the flowers opened to the night, spreading their breath, heated by the kiss of the sun, drinking the refreshing dew that wept into their pale calices. Sensuality floated in the air, dilating panting breasts and inundating them with tumultuous sensations, aphrodisiac dreams that made the nerves vibrate with a frisson anticipating pleasure . . .

Children, all naked, were asleep extended on the paving stones and the steps of porticos. More than once, Naphis felt his mantle tugged by an engaging hand; he tore it away with an abrupt gesture, disgustedly, from the fingers that gripped it. The boldest touches even strayed over his bare legs; he lifted his foot as if to crush a reptile, to the repulsive viscosity of which he had been subjected. He accelerated his pace, went through the triumphal arch erected in honor of Abram, descended along the avenue of Adama to the river and went along the quays all the way to the outlying district of Ze'boim. There he stopped abruptly. The gardens of the temple plunged steeply into the river; beyond them, those of Abimael were staged, likewise bathed by the Iarden.

Naphis is not deterred by that obstacle; he is in a state of exaltation that no human force could restrain.

He launches himself into the bed of the river and abandons himself to its flow. By the light of the moon, which is rising above the horizon, he soon recognizes the clump of lemon trees in which he once perceived Maheleth, pensive, on the day after the evening on which he rescued her. There, at daybreak, he had come to contemplate her from the other bank, invisible for her, masked by a thicket of myrtle-grass.

The bank is sheer; he gropes for some time without being able to come ashore; finally, he clings on to a rocky cleft and attempts to scale it. He raises himself up with difficulty, bruising his knees and bloodying his hands; his tunic, weighed down by water, hinders his movements, paralyzing his efforts; he falls back, exhausted. Irritated, he takes off his garments and, clinging to the rock, throws them over the enclosing hedge, rage multiplying the vigor of his arm tenfold.

He recommences his ascent, even more dolorous for his naked limbs. Sometimes, loosened stones give way under his weight, and the splashes of their fall emerge from the void while he swings momentarily, suspended. He is about to lose strength and courage; he stiffens himself, and, with a supreme thrust of his back, reaches the summit of the cliff. He makes a hole in the spiny cactus and parts the menacing spikes of aloes without paying any heed to their darts. He does not feel anything, except that he is nearing his goal; he can still hear the appeal that invoked him in his insomnia; he goes as straight as a stone launched by the infallible sling of a hunter.

He cannot find his garments. What does his nudity matter? Searching for them would delay his presence next to the person who is waiting for him. For she is waiting; he is sure of it.

With a furtive and muffled step he plunged into the gardens, but his silhouette, projected by the moon, emerging from the top of the tall trees, cut out an enormous shadow on the luminous meadow. He hid in all haste in a clump of lemon-trees—the one where he had seen Maheleth dreaming—and there, he strove to master his hectic thoughts.

A voluptuous breeze bathed him with the sweet scent of iris, dominated by the wilds effluvia of euphorbias and the penetrating exhalations of lilies; over his head, the flowering lemon-trees pour their intoxications; in the shadows, a nightingale modulated its melancholy and passionate scale, and the young man was subject to their forceful impressions; his senses buzzed under the pressure of blood and reared up with desire.

At that moment he was no longer thinking about anything but amour. As he drew closer to the adored, his doubts had dissipated like the vestige of a footprint in the sand of a shore flattened by the caress of the waves, melting like an imprint in snow under the kiss of a sunbeam. Amour was calling to him; he was going to amour . . .

He raised his eyes and looked around in order to orientate his search. The bleak and somber façade of the high priest's palace loomed up before him, as severe as a prison and as menacing as a fortress. The lunar light brightened the blackness of the bituminous walls, which the windows punctuated with duller, denser patches, but less sinister than the shiny tint of the walls.

Naphis contemplated the lugubrious dwelling with a frisson of horror, as if, in a fantastic vision, the grim city of Qain had surged forth before him, the Henokhia whose fabulous history still terrified. He had a chill in his heart on sensing his Maheleth imprisoned in that funereal lair.

But his thought soon traversed the walls and the beloved radiated in a nimbus of dazzling splendor.

Suddenly, a song moaned in the darkness; a plaintive voice wept like a spring trickling over moss, as suppliant as the ululation of a nocturnal bird . . . a sob and a prayer!

The flower of amour germinated in me
Will wither without having bloomed;
It can blossom for one alone,
Or I do not want to be loved.

Goddess of sensuality,
Zirbanit, Zirbanit, my plaint goes to you;
Rather than be Noeph's, inflict the shame
    on me
Of retaining my virginity!

The man for whom my heart languishes
    awaiting,
Zirbanit, is he not your son?
Go tell my plaint to Naphis . . .
I appeal to him . . . he ought to hear me!

You, the lover of the golden stars,
Zirbanit, Zirbanit, O queen of the stars,
If others than Naphis must lift my veils,
Envelop me in death!

To die . . . ! But at that word I tremble;
To die . . . without my life being his
For an hour that would give me to him . . .
To die! Yes, but to die together!

O goddess of lovers,
Zirbanit, Zirbanit, I implore you and
I weep . . .
Only give us one day, only give us an hour,
And we will be able to die happy!

The last sound dies away . . . but then, from the foot of the wall, a stifled voice rises:

"Here I am!"

The sobs stop in the captive's throat; she no longer knows anguish, she has forgotten tears, her eyes and lips only live in order to smile.

"You! You! It's really you . . . ! I love you!"

Then, as if reproaching herself for having thrown to her beloved the first cry of joy and gratitude, she raises her eyes and lifts her hands toward the heavens, where Zirbanit is resplendent among the myriads of stars.

"You have heard my dolor, you have granted my prayer; be blessed, star of amour, O Zirbanit!"

Naphis scrapes his fingernails on the smooth asphalt of the wall; he is exasperated at being so close to his adored and so far from her kiss; he is desperate to get closer to her. He wants to see her, to drown his gaze in hers, to melt into her embrace.

Maheleth is leaning out of the window; the moonlight, playing in the whiteness of her veils, opalizes her face and turns the unkempt tresses of her hair ash-gray; she suddenly recoils, confused and palpitating; Naphis' body, in its pure form, is shining like a bronze idol; she is ecstasized by its beauty, which burns her face, dries her lips and troubles her heart.

Only then does the young man become conscious of his nudity and retreat into the shadow. Makelath unfastens her veil, which twists and comes to settle, like a white turtle-dove, at the pastor's feet. The latter puts it on and wants to attempt a new assault. The virgin stops him.

"Don't exhaust yourself in sterile efforts, my Lord! These walls cannot be scaled. I'm captive and you cannot reach me."

"Captive?"

"Alas! And very unhappy before having heard your voice; the heavens weighed upon my head, impassive and deaf, the world collapsed beneath my feet, my extended arms only grasped the void and I was engulfed in an unfathomable abyss, my eyes blinded by darkness. Now, you are here, there is light, I hope. I am strong, I have faith in the future! Our amour will overcome the obstacles, and defy those who want to separate us."

"It's true, then?"

"My father has not been able to forgive Abram his disdain for my alliance; his hatred envelops everything connected with the Hebrew. He was informed of our meeting on the river bank, and I had to confess everything. At your name he burst forth in imprecations and has ordered me to be Noeph's spouse."

"O rage! Why did you make me spare that wretch?"

"My father hates you," said Maheleth, simply, "but I love you, and I will never belong to anyone but you!"

"Maheleth, my beloved, forgive me! I almost doubted your love. For a few hours, I endured all the pangs of jealousy; an inflamed poison corroded my bones, my brain was unhinged, my swollen heart suffocated when your companion Zogar announced your engagement to the patriarch Lot in front of me."

"It is already known?"

"I did not want to believe it. However, such strange things are said about the daughters of Sodom! But no, you could not be like the others . . . It was necessary for me to see you, to speak to you; I knew that you loved me; in spite of everything, I never ceased to have faith in you, in your love, and, strong in that faith, I have come."

"O my Naphis! I love you!"

"I love you! Maheleth . . ."

"Listen. If my father has spoken, the hour is menacing. Naphis, elect of my soul, save me!"

"I shall save you or die. But speak, inspire me: what can we attempt?"

The virgin absorbed herself in a profound reflection; finally, she said:

"Tomorrow, in the temple, a great sacrifice is being celebrated in honor of Nabou, to render him thanks and conserve his favor for the city purified of barbarians. Although my father is keeping me prisoner, he cannot prevent me from attending it. The place of the daughter of the Great Cohen is at the head of the sacred choirs, and at such a solemnity her absence would be scandalous. Come to the temple, mingle with the crowd, and when it withdraws, profit from the confusion to hide in an obscure corner. Wear simple garments. During the priests' feast I shall be less closely watched; I will try to join you and I hope to succeed. Will you come, my Naphis?"

"Ah!" cried the young man, impetuously.

Maheleth made a fearful gesture; he lowered his voice.

"Yes; even if I had to traverse an army or march over ardent firebrands amid flames, I would be there; I will be there, and we'll flee together. We'll put ourselves under the inviolable protection of Abram. Bara owes his throne and his wealth to him; he venerates him and fears him too much to support your father against him. In any case, who would be able to tear you from my arms while I hold you against my heart? He would remember, that audacious individual, that I am the victor of Hoba! No one would dare! We shall live in the valley of Mamré, united by the benediction of the patriarch, who loves me like the son of his flesh. Nature has refused him children; we shall be his."

"I will flee, I will be cursed by my father . . . I love you, Naphis, I will go wherever your hand guides me. But let us fear the wrath of the gods."

"Our cause is just, and what do your divinities matter? El-Elion, the God of Abram, is the sole master of Heaven and earth; only he is powerful, and he protects us."

"Don't blaspheme my gods, you whom I love! Zirbanit has been compassionate to us . . . oh!" she exclaimed, alarmed. "Look, the sky is darkening; the goddess is testifying her anger to us . . ."

An immense livid cloud surged from the horizon, covering the entire celestial vault, burying the extinct constellations under its dense crepes; in that invasive flux, through a single chink, only Zirbanit sparkled.

"Star of love," Maheleth implored, "do not veil your gaze; smile, smile again; do not abandon us!"

But the clouds were still flowing, shrinking the azure bay; the planet remained alone, like a golden nail on a funerary drape; then it threw forth a vacillating ray, the last, and sank into the darkness. Up above, in the firmament, and down below, on the earth, only an unfathomable night reigned any longer.

Maheleth was devastated. Zirbanit was withdrawing from them; all was lost . . . She wept.

"Have faith in El-Elion," Naphis repeated. "Have faith in our amour!"

And that cry rose up so full and so confident that it penetrated the heart of the virgin of Sodom. She repressed her tears, and, putting all her soul into her words, she murmured:

"Yes, I have faith, Naphis; the faith that is yours and makes me yours. Your fatherland, your family and your God are my fatherland, my family and my God!"

Then, as if to consecrate the impulse of her heart and the gift of her being, to give him a pledge of divine benediction, a great breath passed through the ether, sweeping away the clouds, and the purified firmament was resplendent again in its magnificence . . .

X

NAPHIS had reentered Lot's palace without the latter having suspected his absence. There he threw himself down on his couch, succumbing to the multiple emotions that had assailed him; soon, he fell asleep: the reparative slumber that nature dispenses to youth, even in the most poignant phases of life. Youth is like the halcyon, which sleeps during the tempest on the bristling crests of the foamy waves.

At daybreak the patriarch, respecting his guest's slumber, set forth to visit his fields and his flocks, in order to honor Naphis with the first fruits of his crops and the flower of his produce. He took his wife with him and recommended the young man that Abram loved to the care of his daughters.

Toward the seventh hour of the night, Zogar, agitated by her desire, had got up surreptitiously in order to go and surprise Naphis in the confused ideas an abrupt awakening and provoke his passion by means of the tempting offering of her radiant nudity. She believed that her sister was asleep and drew away cautiously; infidel to the oath made, she wanted to be the first, if not the only one, to conquer the amour of the superb pastor.

Radja had preceded her. She found her, stupefied, standing before the empty bed.

The two sisters measured one another with their gaze. Radja extinguished beneath her eyelids the hateful glare that Zogar's perfidy had ignited in her. Grimly, her younger sister upset the mats, lacerating the fabric, trampling them with her feet and accumulating on them her impotent rage. Guttural exclamations were strangled in her larynx or hissed through her teeth, clenched by rage.

Nervously, she vented her suppressed desire and her overflowing anger. Then she let herself fall on the disordered fleeces, biting them in a full mouth, not knowing whether she was seeking a further vengeance or slaking her appetite for the male with the impregnated odor of the man. Finally, exhausted, she writhed in a nervous crisis and stiffened, inertly.

Calmer but no less wounded, Radja meditated. Somber and creased to begin with, her forehead soon relaxed and brightened.

"Fool," she said, darting an ironic glance at her sister. "Maheleth is being kept prisoner by Abimael; what does it matter to us if Naphis goes to prowl around the temple? He can't reach her, and in three days our rival's marriage will be consummated. The cohen swore it to us by Nabou. I won't belie our agreement, Zogar, even though you've attempted to violate it tonight; if you want to listen to me, to follow my advice and let me act, Naphis will be swooning in our arms this very day."

"Truly?" cried Zogar, sitting up ardently.

"I guarantee it, if you submit to my will."

"Anything, anything . . . I swear it!"

"Calm down and listen."

Radja drew her sister away, after having put their guest's bed in order. Once extended beside one another in the gynaeceum, she spoke; she spoke for a long time. Anxiously, Zogar devoured her words. Finally, when Radja fell silent, she leapt to her feet, exclaiming:

"To work! He's ours!"

※

When he awoke, Naphis passed his hand over his forehead, rendered heavy by the reaction of his nocturnal fatigue, in order to expel the fog therefrom. He paraded a wandering gaze around him. On a stool beside his bed was a cup full of aromatized wine, the sweet perfume of which attracted his lips. He extended his arm, seized it, bore it to his mouth and emptied it in a single draught. Then he fell back upon the cushions and was progressively invaded by a delectable languor.

In the cool penumbra of the apartment he abandoned himself to the wellbeing of his soft bed and the mildly embalmed moisture emitted by its wool, sprinkled with iris. His weary and bruised limbs stretched voluptuously; the nervous overexcitement of his insomnia and the heavy exhaustion of his slumber gave way to a soothing relaxation that soon lulled him in a vague reverie . . .

. . . Today; it's today that he must see his beloved again, conquer her forever, take her in his arms, carry away his treasure . . . ! Maheleth! It seems to him that he did not exist before knowing her, that his life commenced with his amour . . .

The hour approaches . . . The temple opens before him . . . Lost in the crowd, he hoists himself up and his gaze wanders over the moving heads, as if over an agitated sea; he seeks the expected image. Nothing yet . . . Ceding to his amour, with a great cry, he summons her . . .

At his evocation she appears, aureoled with light, in the aerial transparency of her floating veils . . . He sinks into mute contemplation, rises up, swims in the air that brushes him, while his feet are riveted to the ground. He struggles desperately, feeling imprisoned in the vice with which the multitude grips him; he strives in vain to cleave through the compact tide; only his soul takes flight, his body struggling in an inextricable net.

The sacred chants unfurl their sonorous waves, floating over the people at prayer, bending their heads as a tempest forces proud palm trees to sweep the sand with their proud tresses under the impetuosity of its gusts . . . Man humiliates himself and God commands . . . Now the voices are deafening, weeping the plaint of the desolate city: a cry burst forth, piercing the air with a clamor of suppliant agony . . . but while its echo is still vibrating, a rumor rises, bursting forth in triumphant acclamations, cries of joy and liberty, and then, in its formidable crescendo, lets the gods speak.

In the incoherence of his dream, a single voice soon dominates the tempest of the choir . . . it stands out as pure as the ring of gold on marble paving stones, as supreme as the bellowing of the shopharoth in the noise of battle . . . and Naphis no longer hears anything else. Strangely enough, that air awakens a memory in him, imposes itself on his thought like the distant echo of the song that cradles our childhood.

His lips seek the words, hesitantly, and gradually murmur:

> *O goddess of lovers,*
> *Zirbanit, Zirbanit, I implore you and*
> *   I weep . . .*
> *Only give us one day, only give us an hour,*
> *And we will be able to die happy!*

He remembers . . . it is the appeal of the adored!

The song has ceased . . . In the deserted temple shadow and silence reign . . . the lights are extinct . . . he is alone.

It is the hour!

The awaited hour . . . the hour that will mark deliverance, the hour that ought to open the era of amour and liberty!

He tried to get up. A torpor numbed his head, paralyzed his limbs; his arms beat the air and fell back, inert. Luminous waves whirled before his eyes, blinding his pupils with a fog striped with sparks that fluttered behind his heavy eyelids . . .

His lips stammered . . . In vain, he struggled, anguished by his impotence; everything crumbled around him, fleeing his contact . . . he seemed to be engulfed in a vertiginous fall, descending, always descending, toward a gulf that was sucking him in . . . when, suddenly, he rose again toward the empyrean, as if the Kherubim had lent him their indefatigable wings . . .

. . . In a halo woven from a dust of stars, an aerial form advanced . . . Its vaporous silhouette sketched adorable lines beneath the transparent delicacy of fabrics; they developed more harmoniously still in the soft inflexions of its seductive stride . . .

It came toward him . . .

Naphis felt his heart leap and fly away from his breast . . . His dream was alive!

She is there, she touches him . . . and as, ecstasized, he adores that incarnation of beauty, blurred in its nebulous diaphaneity, the veil quivers, opens, flies away . . . the radiant flesh is manifest in its apotheosis . . . two soft and febrile arms encircle his neck; two absorbing lips drink his lips; two breasts are crushed upon his chest and penetrate it with their victorious reverberation. He delights in the embalmed breath that breathes an inexhaustible desire into him . . .

Tongues of flame lick his loins; he loves their exquisite burn; impetuous blood flows in his arteries, swelling them as if to burst in an imminent deflagration; an unknown vigor clenches his fibers, while his brain is liquefied in boiling lava . . . His arid mouth exhausts itself in kisses, his muscular arms are knotted in an inflexible contraction . . . limbs are linked, bodies are welded . . . under the persistent effort the obstacle cedes . . . An intense vibration shakes their two doubled beings simultaneously . . . Swooning, the espoused abandons herself; he, still seeking kisses, stirs convulsively in the void, his lips fluttering over clenched teeth . . .

Everything collapses . . . a prostration of infinite languor, of celestial suavity, numbs Naphis, wadding him in the annihilation of the collected sensuality . . .

Next to the united couple a woman is standing. A spasmodic agitation causes her teeth to chatter, her hands are wringing with impatience, anger and desire. Those two lovers, there before her, cause an upheaval in her thought. She hates the other who has anticipated her, enraged to have ceded her place to her. She leans over, her fingers clench on the shoulder of the palpitating woman stuck to Naphis' lips and she shoves her away with a savage thrust, like that of the paw of a wild beast, strips off her tunic and slides in her place against the loins of the handsome pastor.

It is Zogar, demanding from her sister the engagement made.

Radja, in her intoxication, resigns herself, quivering, to yielding the man she has made her own. She is thirsty for further caresses and new spasms; the enjoyment savored has rendered her body more insatiable; exhausted of sensuality, it is still strong enough for a similar crush . . . but the struggle is impossible; it would betray their ruse and might provoke a lucidity that would dissipate Naphis' illusion.

In order to be alone in having possessed him, she would consent to reveal her trap; would not the joy given absolve her in the shepherd's heart? Exhausted by enjoyment, however, she only has strength for amour! Zogar has pushed her away, menacing, superb in passion and tension; she feels vanquished, recoils and collapses among the cushions.

Naphis, his eyes closed, sighs . . . his lips palpitate in an incoherent appeal . . . his arms extend

138

and close in a new enlacement; more warm kisses stimulate a further powerful desire in him . . . and Zogar knows amour . . . !

✳

The hours go by . . .

Noisily, the people of Sodom converge in the direction of the temple, flooding over the parvis, crowding and accumulating there. The priests bring toward the sacrificial slab the victims that are to fall on the altar of Nabou: ewes with wool dyed scarlet, adorned with floating ribbons; rams and he-goats with gilded horns and pelts shiny with cinnamon; bulls and heifers newly adult, having not yet engendered or conceived.

The iobel releases its sonorous note, which unleashes the resounding fanfare of tympanons and cymbals; amid their blasts the fearful bleatings and formidable bellowings are dissonant. The Great Cohen advances, draped in a mehil of violet wool twice plunged into the dyers' vats, girdled by a crimson sash with long floating ends.

Every step, taken in slow and solemn cadence, caused the fringes to undulate and the little golden bells that festooned the edge of the mehil to ring. From the belt rose the ephod of fine twisted linen, over which the bright colors of crimson and hyacinth shone. The shoulder-pads were fastened by two bezels of gold of Ophir, each holding a sardonyx, on each of which was engraved the cabalistic sign of Nabou, god of Sodom.

Two gold chains attached to the clasps supported the zodion, charged with gems tracing the sacred characters with their sewing. On the head of the high priest the mizenophet was staged, from which a long veil of diaphanous fabric hung down.

Abimael was followed by his assessors, carrying incense in cassolettes of Ophir, myrrh on silver trays and the sacrificial knife on a crimson carpet.

The victims fell under the sacrificer's blade; their entrails fumed on the bloody altar; songs burst forth triumphantly and the harmony of the sacred choirs ecstasized the crowd.

Then the ceremony came to an end and the people withdrew, everyone running impatiently to the orgies for which every festival was merely the pretext for a frantic recrudescence.

The priests had gone to the hall of the feast where the delicate portions of the victims awaited them, along with honey-cakes, wines of Arba and lotus liqueurs. They went avidly to the revelry that would commence their drunkenness and prepare their excesses . . .

Without difficulty, Maheleth has deceived the surveillance of her guardians, who are taking advantage of the general relaxation in order to glean their share of joy. Alone with her faithful Basemath she slips into the temple and searches its nooks and crannies . . .

Naphis is not at the rendezvous!

She waits. The minutes go by, slow and cruel; the minutes are succeeded by hours . . . Naphis has not come! Naphis is not coming!

Devastated, she falls into her nurse's arms, sobbing. No more hope . . . ! She does not accuse her beloved, oh no! It is for that reason that an atrocious anguish is clawing her heart. If Naphis is absent, it is because of an insurmountable cause.

She shivers . . . she senses that her father is capable of anything . . . must she wear mourning for her fiancé already?

Worried by their prolonged wait and the dolorous state of Maheleth, Basemath takes her away. The virgin yields without resistance, unconsciously. She returns to her apartments, and there collapses in a despairing agony . . .

Then the door of the temple opened, and Naphis appeared, pale and haggard.

XI

NAPHIS has woken up, his head heavy, numbed by the vapors of his long intoxication, his body exhausted by its spasms. His confused thoughts drift; his squinting eyes paraded around him the emptiness of a gaze that suddenly comes to life, fixing in a horrified stupor . . .

There, close by, amid the chaotic mass of mats and hides, two naked forms are displaying their lascivious languor, their exhaustion of sated females, in a heavy slumber . . . Radja and Zogar! His host's daughters . . . Immediately, the visions of his dream are designed before him . . . the veil tears . . . the last clouds evaporate . . . he understands . . . he understands everything.

Heartbroken, he lets his forehead fall into the palms of his clenched hands; he rends his flesh and tears out his hair. Then an idea traverses his mind; his rendezvous? Already the sun has completed more than half its course . . . Is he too late?

With one bound he is on his feet and has put on his traveling clothes; hatefully, he steps over the voluptuous bodies lying at his feet, with a desire to flagellate them, to ravage their beauty with his fingernails: those bodies that he has possessed treasonously; and he presses the ground with his heel, turning it, as if he were crushing the head of a maleficent viper; then he goes out, spitting behind him scornfully, wiping his lips angrily.

He cannot forgive those young women for having caused him to prostitute his amour. He does not know whether he is suffering more from the peril that his delay might cause, or from no longer having to give to his Maheleth a body as virginal as his heart. His anger is all the greater because his recent pleasures have been so intense. He would like to forget them, and yet their obsession haunts him. He denies them but still shudders with them . . . Oh, how good it would be to avenge himself, if the hour were not so pressing! But he has already waited too long . . . ! And he starts running toward the temple.

He races, burning the paving stones, splitting his sandals in the urgency of the bounds that vigorous spring of his hamstrings precipitate. The walls flee around him, the whipped air labors his lungs . . . he goes on . . . and on . . .

Finally, he arrives.

The fronton of the temple, figurant in gold and bloody with jasper, displayed the sacred sign of the god of Sodom, the monogram of Nabou, framed by two Kherubim with the hairy bodies of bulls, the outspread wings of eagles and human faces, one brandishing a flaming sword, the other singing to the gods on an ivory kinnor with seven bronze strings.

The parvis, paved with white marble with pink veins, extended before the sanctuary; broad steps ran along the entire façade, forming the substratum of the edifice and crowned with a bold colonnade of red porphyry, the pillars of which surpassed forty cubits, the entablature and the cornices being a sanguine jasper streaked with gold. At the summit, a balustrade of solid gold, superbly sculpted, dominated the temple and surmounted it like a diadem. The peristyle was paved by a mosaic of inestimable workmanship. Doors of cedar-wood, fretted with silver, gave access to the public enclosure.

The interior paneling was in oiled olive-wood framed with shittim moldings; along three faces stood a range of enormous rectangular columns, in which sections of jasper, cornelian and onyx alternated from one cubit to the next, with circular golden sutures. Only the area between the pillars and the wall was covered, with a ceiling of cypress jointed with steel lamina.

The temple faced eastwards, constructed and disposed in accordance with the traditions of the Tower of Babel. Above the south-western corner a bronze mare reared up in memory of Tubalcain and Ham, whose races had populated the land of Khoush; to the north-west, the prow of a ship in shittim wood recalled Noah's ark, according to the Hebrews, or that of Xisouthris, claimed the men of the Chaldean race, which had survived the deluge and run aground in the Gordyoen Mountains; to the north-east, an iron kherub guarded the road to Eden with his flaming sword; and to the south-east a gold elephant raised its bronze trunk and its ivory tusks, Each of those emblems sustained a corner of the immense scarlet awning, dyed by two immersions in the vats. Two cubits above, a tent was deployed made of stitched ewe-skins, dyed violet, which from zereth to zereth, was held taut by a bronze buttress.

In the center sloped a porphyry bath that over-hung onyx basins; jets of scented water broke up therein and were vaporized in a perfumed mist. On ivory pedestals, incense, amber and galbanum were fuming in cassolettes of Ophir gold. At the back, a crimson paroketh was draped, veiling from profane gazes the mishkan and the sacrificial altar.

Then the sanctuary rounded out in a curve, from which numerous galleries radiated, entwining like a labyrinth and distributing the apartments of the cohanim, their banquet halls and their hearths of debauchery. There lived the priests of Nabou, ordinarily careless of sacrifices. They lustered their hair and beards with cinnamon and perfumed their lips with myrrh; lying on cool mats of palm-leaves, rendered softer by the sheepskins piled up beneath them, they allowed their tunics of fine linen embroidered with hyacinth and sown with bright gemstones, float over their semi-nudity.

They spent their hours languorously in the enervating atmosphere of the temple, not fearing to deliver themselves there to the most execrable excesses. A young slave, crouching at their feet, was ever ready to anticipate and content their desires. Into the sacred enclosure, where only they could penetrate without sacrilege, they nevertheless introduced the virgins and ephebes of the city, seduced by their promises or acquired by the most odious abductions, and the lamps of the divine rites illuminated their abominations . . .

✳

As he penetrated under the parvis, out of breath by virtue of the rapidity of his course and tortured by anxiety, Naphis used both his hands to compress his heart, which was beating feverishly, as if to burst through his breast. His menaced amour made his loins tremble like those of a young bride at the first shock that reveals her living maternity to her. The beneficent shade bathed his forehead, burned by the torrid heat that the sun poured over the breathless earth and enfevered by his night of deceptive amours, with a delectable coolness.

Like the streets, the temple was empty; at that hour everyone was seeking repose, lying on woven reeds next to spurting fountains, breathing in the air refreshed by their soothing humidity.

Naphis stops. Gradually, the calm and well-being that descend from the high walls and the double awning moderate the seething of his blood and render clarity to his thought. Although the public enclosure in deserted, the perfumes are still exhaling their effluvia, so the end of the ceremony must be recent. Maheleth has not come yet; he hopes so, and wants to believe it.

He slides from pillar to pillar, sounding the obscure corners, and reaches the Paroketh that veils the entrance to the mishkan, the holy place reserved for the cohanim. He parts the curtains . . . No one!

Boldly, he advances, passing before the table of offerings, lifts another curtain and emerges from the sanctuary. He finds himself in the vault into which the maze of corridors opens. At hazard, Naphis ventures into their network. Everywhere there is silence and solitude. He plunges further forward . . . Maheleth is summoning him, he wants to reach Maheleth.

He fears now that she might be waiting for him in the public enclosure; he retraces his steps, goes astray, persists in his search, his soul compressed by his anguish and his heart bruised in its amour. Oh, how he reproaches himself now for his intoxication; how he hates those who have abused his deceptive dreams!

He emerges into a vast hall, bizarrely holed by alcoves in which piles of cushions and beds of furs are drowned in the shadow of heavy opaque curtains. Mats and soft carpets are rounded out in front of those obscure niches, which sweat shame and retain the insipid reek of their leprous soilings, in spite of the aphrodisiac perfumes burning on the tripods, the smoke of which spreads in opaline spirals that trail in the air like a blossoming of prurience. Naphis is in the mysterious redoubt where the cohanim conduct their infamous fornications.

A noise of songs and laughter, muffled at first, reaches his ears and is magnified, drawing nearer. Bewildered, he takes refuge in the nearest alcove and hides behind its thick curtains. The creases, violently parted, fall back, stiffened by their weight . . . just in time. The doors open.

Tottering, their faces congested, the priests advance, each sustained by his ephebe, whose nudity is ornamented with jewels, like that of a prostitute. Negroes from the land of Khoush, stolen from the cradle and raised for their usage in the depths of the temple, have bronzed skin, shiny with oil. Their white teeth laugh behind the vivid flesh of their fleshy lips, which resemble the edges of a bloody wound. Some of them only show pink gums, having had their jaws stripped, a barbarity invented to render their caresses softer. Their plump rumps have a waddle that renders more lubricious the parting of their thighs in their slow and sickly march. The children of the white race are more obese; the sedentary life, the lack of air and the nourishment on which they are gorged swell their thighs with fatty creases and make their bellies balloon; their breasts are swollen like the teats of a young virgin. Some are castrated and owe a more deformed corpulence to their mutilation.

They aid their masters to lie down on their beds of repose, pile cushions behind their heads, and, crouching beside them within range of their whims, for which their eyes, like those of recumbent dogs, appear to be begging, and which their caressant fingers seek to provoke.

Abimael's hand plays negligently with the curly blond hair spiraling over the gracile shoulders of a beautiful androgyne, whose double sex, amusing his blasé appetites, receives and returns his caresses alternately . . . Then, after a yawn of satiety, he stretches himself and strikes a silver cymbal with his fist.

At the back of the room the curtains are parted. A strange music emits slow and grave sounds, through which pass drunken sobs and infernal sniggers; then the cadence accelerates, shrill notes burst forth and the movement becomes precipitate . . .

Naked, their wrists and ankles circled with gold and their throats streaming with necklaces, the head alone enveloped in an aerial and diaphanous scarf, dancers irrupt into the hall, gliding on tiptoe, their hamstrings taut. Soon they flex; the heels draw closer together, the knees part, the quivering thighs open; their backs accentuate their arch increasingly, causing the bellies to protrude, which roll voluptuously as the hips bounce. Now they are all in a line, shoulder to shoulder, linking their softly thrown arms in a weave of flesh.

The enraged rhythm slows; they exaggerate the pose, leaning backwards in a bold release, their heels under the buttocks, their kneecaps thrown sideways, extending their mystic rose, flamboyant on the depilated flesh.

Their heads, tipped back, mingle the somber or tawny reflections of their tresses; they oscillate with a progressive sway that makes breasts and bellies turbulent, inflated as if in the possession of a male.

The iobel emits a strident note . . . With a somersault they straighten up again, resuming their swaying march, still advancing, more indecently, brushing the faces of the cohanim with their moist skin, which heightens the perfumes with which it is anointed with the spice of its carnal exhalations. But the priests scarcely have a dull radiance in their blasé gaze, accustomed to that spectacle, or a frisson in their bodies, saturated by such fornications. Again, Abimael makes the cymbals collide. The dancers run away laterally; swooning, wearied by the enjoyment that their own excitation has provoked, still vibrant without being sated, they collapse on the fleeces piled along the walls.

The ephebes appear in their turn. They are no longer the pitiful atrophied individuals attached to the person of the priests but young adults, svelte and delicately muscled, with supple limbs and an elegant gait. Nothing interrupts their superb nudity, the ivory polish of their bright skin, made supple by oily unguents.

The eyes of the cohanim are awakened, bestial smiles returning to their slack lips. These dancers are truly beautiful.

Abimael is triumphant. These slaves come from northern regions, where his emissaries have recruited them at great expense. Their eunuchs were able to hide them during the invasion in the secret subterrains of the temple. Their presence in Sodom was only known to the Great Cohen. Today he is exhibiting them, instructed in their art and resplendent in their beauty.

But an atrocious cruelty has marred them; the approach of a hot iron beneath the eyelids has vitrified their pupils—a precaution taken to avoid their union with the hetaerae, who contemplate them avidly in their ever-excited but rarely satisfied lust.

Guided by their eunuchs, the dancers take their places in the arena where they are to deploy their agile talents and plastic poses. Their chief plays a prelude on the kinnor and they all undulate in unison, their arms raised, swaying alternately from one side to the other, accompanying their rocking with harmonious flexions of the torso. The amplitude of the oscillations increases, the head of each one coming to caress the hip of his neighbor, and at each contact it brushes it with a lascivious kiss. Arms parted, lowered, glide over shoulders and come to link torsos with a girdle of interlaced flesh; two by two, mouths seek one another, encounter one another and retain one another.

The chain is broken; the couples remain united. Tightly welded, they simulate the pleasures of lust; then the groups climb up on one another's shoulders, building a human pyramid that seems to be shaken by the same erotic folly, which quivers in the same spasm.

A hectic hymn rises, borne by the bronze strings of kinnors, modulated by the hoarse outbursts of buccinas, the bellowing of tympanons and the clash of cymbals; the oarystis of Zirbanit bellows like an orgiastically unleashed squall . . .

Pour your intoxication in floods into our cups,
Let male and female unite their troops
Around our heads coupled in groups
To charm the eyes;

Zirbanit! Singing your solemn laws,
To you, whose amours vibrate eternally,
We consecrate our carnal hours
Of lustfulness!

154

Here, we give you the ingenuous virgin,
The exalting ephebe closes his naked flesh;
They are going to savor the unknown ecstasy
In our muscular arms.

We reserve for them the intimate kisses;
If they die amid the ultimate pleasures
On your golden altar, our beautiful victims
Will tell you our prayers.

Zirbanit, descend from your empyrean,
The tithe of amour desired by you
And the blood wetting the flesh torn
By a powerful rut . . .

Ah, we exalt you by our dementia;
Zirbanit, descend, your fête commences,
Our libations are our semen
Drowned in their blood!

A few had raised themselves up, but, heavy
with wine and meat, they fell back on their mats,
their artificial desire already dead. Only the pupils
of the hetaerae were dilated, fascinated by the
rut of the ephebes, which their nudity displayed
freely. Those young men, in spite of their blindness, sensed the gazes riveted upon them, they
divined the presence of women by the emanations

of their being, and the same desire haunted them; a dull irritation fermented in the double troop, overflowing with youth, which had for its destiny to foment the amour that is forbidden to them!

In the revolt of their puberty, the adults were already putting their feverish hands on themselves and yielding to their interior torment . . . That was too much! In the blink of an eye the hetaerae understood, and in a single surge, rushed upon the troop of males. There was a formidable collision of plastered flesh, enraged kisses, sobs, cries, crumpled muscles, the cracking of bones . . . In vain the eunuchs had run forward; their weak hands could not break the embraces; their whips, striping the bodies with red furrows, far from making them release their prey, enraged them further. Howls of pain were stifled by the gasps of orgasm; and when they were separated, the unsated tongues were still licking the blood that hands had taken from the wounds!

That strange melee, that human torrent whose floods were limbs in frenetic contortion, had revived a spark in the atony of the cohanim. But Abimael did not want to compromise in a single occasion the enormous sums that the harem had cost the temple treasure. He had given the order to interrupt that unusual spectacle of refinement and horror.

The priests murmured; one of them even stood up, his robe open, proud of his reconquered virility, and cried: "More!"

That cry shook the most somnolent to their marrow. Instantly, they were all upright, gesticulating and howling: "More! More!"

They pressed around the impassive and disdainful Abimael, imploring him or abusing him . . . The Great Cohen remained deaf; the most enraged made a menacing gesture; slowly, Abimael raised his arm and sent the audacious individual sprawling on the paving-stones by striking him on the head with his ivory staff.

They all recoiled, tamed. Their attempted revolt had already exhausted their ephemeral flame. They had abused their delirious lusts and saguinary debauchery to such an extent that the pleasure offered no longer tempted them. They had only been whipped by the unexpectedness of that spontaneous melee. Abimael understood that. They required the stimulus of the unexpected, of the impossible. He did not want to rest on the failure of his authority, momentarily misunderstood and subsequently shaken; it was necessary to create for them, immediately, an extravagant monstrosity.

An infernal idea germinates in his brain, condenses through the fumes of intoxication, takes form, grows and solidifies.

He gives the order to fetch Maheleth!

At that name, Naphis, in his hiding-place, stupefied by fear until then, shudders in horror. Maheleth, his fiancée, his pure amour, in that place of orgy! He thinks he has misheard.

But to the sound of kitharas the virgin advances, dragged by the eunuchs of the gynaeceum. A fearful gaze runs from her father to the crowd and then returns, suppliant and condemnatory, to fix on Abimael.

He sustains the mute reproach of her eyes, causes them to lower under the steely glare of his own, and speaks to her: will she consent to be Noeph's wife?

"Never!" she responds, proudly, raising her head, the veil of which parts and allows the immutable resolution imprinted on her features to be seen.

"You're resisting my will? Be careful!"

"Never!"

"You are no longer my child; I give you to the goddess. Eunuchs, strip her of her garments—and you, daughter of Zirbanit, dance before us!"

The cohanim applaud.

Already, the trembling slaves are raising their hands to her garments. Maheleth pushes them away with a gesture, marches straight to her father and, superb with indignation, looking him in the face, eye to eye, says:

"Dare, then!"

Mad with rage, exasperated by that new challenge to his authority, the resistance that insults him publicly, and then immediately brought back to his obscene conceptions by his daughter's beauty, Abimael, intoxicated by lust, howled:

"Naked, naked! I want her completely naked. You'll dance, under the whip if you resist, and afterwards . . . afterwards . . ."

His throat choked; foam flecked the corners of his mouth; brutally, his hand ripped away Mahaleth's veil and laid her breasts bare.

The virgin uttered a cry of anguish, to which a formidable roar responded; cleaving through the crowd, knocking over the eunuchs, Naphis came to a halt before her . . .

Maheleth held out her arms; heedless of the peril, without seeing imminent death, Naphis took her upon his heart, and their lips drank their kiss!

A stupor reigned over the assembly . . . a fearful silence . . . a hateful silence . . . a deathly silence . . .

The devastating intervention of Naphis had struck the crowd with a superstitious terror; stupefied, the cohanim had recoiled; the eunuchs, flat on the ground, muttered prayers; the hetaerae adored the god who had revealed himself.

"Death!" roared Abimael. "Death to the Hebrew, the impious individual who has violated our enclosure, the sacrilegious individual who has surprised our mysteries; his blood is due to our gods!"

And the cohanim, standing up, haggard, saliva on their teeth and their eyes bloodshot, vociferated "Death! Death!"

Arms came down, breaking the lovers' embrace; knocked down and tied up, Naphis was carried impotently to the altar. His lacerated garments flew away and the young man was manifest in his splendor of a demigod.

Cupid eyes no longer saw anything but his beauty. Abimael felt himself stirred by an atrocious desire. Kill him? No! He would take a better vengeance!

"Stop!" he cried, throwing away the sacrificial knife. "Take them away . . . imprison them in the subterrains of the temple . . . I consecrate them to the service of the gods."

With a filthy smile he leaned over the convulsed face of the captive; Naphis closed his eyes. Abimael approached the seal of his ring to the flame of a tripod, and applied it, red-hot, to the forehead of the victor of Hoba. The flesh sizzled and the ideographic sign of Nabou blazed in bloody streaks on the face of the victim!

Maheleth had fainted . . .

XII

FAR away in the verdant valley, under the large and leafy crown of the oak that sheltered his tent, Abram watched the sun sink toward the horizon with a dull gaze and a pensive expression. The patriarch's thought was in Sodom, following Naphis, the handsome adolescent whom he loved.

Since the day when the young pastor had accompanied him to his tent the Hebrew had not lamented as much the sterility of his wife Saraï; his heart had directed all his feelings of paternal affection to his son of election. Yes, his thought was in Sodom, since Sodom possessed Naphis.

A sheaf of anxious wrinkles converged on his forehead and inscribed a somber line in the contraction of his eyebrows, making the coarse bushy tufts bristle. Abram let his white-haired head fall heavily on to his breast. He was thinking about the posterity that Elohim refused him.

Saraï, ashamed of her sterility, had had thrown into the patriarch's couch his maidservant Agar, a beautiful Egyptian given to him when barely nubile by the Pharaoh on their departure from the land of Mizraim, when the king returned to the Hebrew the wife that the Book of the Dead forbade him to keep. Agar had conceived of Abram, had given birth to Ismael, and, in her maternal pride had looked at her mistress insolently. Saraï had demanded and obtained the exile of the superb slave. Now the patriarch remained alone, beside an old and morose woman, without the son of his flesh and without the son of his heart . . .

What cause was prolonging Naphis' sojourn in Sodom for so long? The attraction of lust? Certainly not! The young man's heart was too pure and his mores too chaste. Amour? Abram divined it and smiled. He had already thought of it in leaving Naphis under Lot's roof. Radja and Zogar were beautiful; the man who was awakening in the adolescent should not have remained insensible to their charm and youth; furthermore, he had saved them.

Abram wanted that marriage, which would unite the Gamoran with him even more narrowly by bonds of blood. But the smile evoked by that hope only wandered over the patriarch's mouth, which resumed its bleak rigidity. A persistent anxiety, as irrational as a presentiment, oppressed his soul; and his gaze turned mechanically toward the road to Sodom, as if to appeal to the absentee.

The sun reached the summit of the hills, biting their erect breasts with its crimson lips and inundating them with a more intense stream of light before sinking into the profundity of the sea. Suddenly, it paused in its decrease; its inflamed face took on life and a thunderous voice exploded in space, rolling its sonorous echoes; the Hebrew prostrated himself, his forehead in the dust, in order to adore Elohim, who was manifesting himself . . .

The voice proclaimed:

"I am the Almighty, the creator and organizer of worlds; I have drawn your body from the mud of the earth; my breath has created your soul from a reflection of my eternity. March before me and be perfect. In spite of your innate humility, I grant you my alliance. I will multiply your race in all the centuries of centuries."

Abram, his arms extended and his face to the ground, murmured:

"I hear your words, Lord, and I have faith in your promises."

"It is your God who is making himself heard; it is your God who is making alliance with a man; you will be the father of numerous peoples. You will no longer name yourself the elevated Father but the Father of the multitude, not Abram but Abraham. I have established for you a host of nations issued of your race; and that race I will multiply infinitely; your blood will command the peoples and give them kings.

"I repeat to you that I have put on you and your descendants the seal of my divine alliance; it will be affirmed there in the succession of time, from generation to generation, and that eternal pact makes me your only God, the sole God of your posterity. As a sign of our union, all the males of your blood will be circumcised. You will circumcise the child in his flesh eight days after his birth, and not only the male children of your families but those of your servants and your slaves. Any uncircumcised man among you will have violated my alliance; he will be stoned in the midst of his people and by his people. Henceforth you will no longer call your wife 'my princess,' but '*the* princess': Sara and not Saraï. My benediction will descend into her entrails and dissolve her sterility; she will give birth to a son, a chief of nations, the root of a line of kings."

Involuntarily, Abraham sensed a smile of incredulity rising to his lips; fearing the anger of the Shaddai, he repressed it. But a child! To have a child of an old woman previously sterile . . . ?

Nothing escapes the omnipresent gaze of the Almighty. Elohim penetrated all the thought of the Hebrew and made his words heard again.

"Sara will have a son by virtue of my omnipotence. You will name him Izehacq,[1] laughter, for you have laughed, and that child will be, after you, the depository of my alliance. Do not delay in executing my orders. My hand will withdraw from those of your people who are not circumcised when the sun has set three times more. I will send you two messengers to go to announce my commandments to those of your family. Remember my words and I will multiply your sons and the sons of your sons more than the stars of the firmament and the grains of sand on the shores. All the nations of the earth will be blessed in you."

Abraham, no longer hearing the voice of the Lord, raised his head. The sun had sunk abruptly behind the hills; the night was gradually invad-

---

1 Izehaq (*sic*) is recorded as the "true name" of Isaac in one of the supplements to Pierre Larousse's *Grand dictionnaire universal*, published in 1877. The version given here is probably a misprint, as the name is rendered as Larousse gives it subsequently.

ing the sky in broad flowing sheets and shrouding the earth with its confused crepes. By his side the Hebrew perceived two men with silhouettes so white in the shadow that they seemed luminous; they were unknown to him.

They spoke: "We are the messengers sent to you by Elohim."

Abraham bent down toward the ground, kissed their knees and introduced them into his tent. When water had been heated over the fire he washed their feet himself and then anointed them with the purest oil; Sara served them unleavened bread, fruits and milk.

After the meal, the two envoys of Heaven got up, refusing nocturnal hospitality, and, furnished with the patriarch's instructions, they set forth for Sodom.

At daybreak the shopharoth summoned all Abram's servants around the oak of Mamré. The Master manifested the celestial will to them, and was the first to be circumcised with a fragment of sharpened flint. All the males of his house did likewise. Then they cauterized their wounds with the white juice of the fig-tree.

Evening came; the messengers had not returned. The night went by slowly for Abraham's insomnia, undermined by the fever of expectation and the fever of the operation he had undergone. The day dawned, increased and declined . . .

Nothing again!

Then Abraham addressed himself to the Lord.

The Almighty spoke:

"I have nothing hidden for the man to whom I have granted my alliance. The abominations of Sodom cry out for vengeance; my envoys will tell me whether I ought to suspend my punishment, but my imminent wrath is floating over the fornicating cities."

"Lord," Abraham implored, trembling for his nephew, and in particular for Naphis, will you doom the just with the impious?"

God did not respond.

"Sovereign Master," the patriarch persisted, "you who judge worlds in your impeccable justice, will you confound the good and the wicked? If, in the culpable city, your messengers find fifty just men, will they perish with the sinners? Will you condemn them with the city, or will you pardon Sodom in their favor?"

Elohim listened to the words of his servant.

"Fifty just men in Sodom will earn the pardon of the city."

"I dare to implore my Lord again," said Abraham, emboldened by the divine benevolence. "I dare to address myself to him, although I am nothing but dust and ash. If five just men are lacking to make up the number, will you doom Sodom?"

"No; forty-five just men will redeem the city."

"Don't punish my audacity, Lord—what will your verdict be if Sodom only counts forty good men?"

"I will spare it."

"Do not impute my persistence to crime, O Omnibenevolent; what if the just only number thirty?"

"I will be merciful."

"You are listening favorably to my prayer; will you still welcome it if there are only twenty?"

"I will grant mercy, at the request of my servant."

"Listen to me one last time, Lord, and it will be my supreme invocation. If there are ten just men in Sodom, will you condemn it?"

"I will forgive."

With that word of clemency, Elohim disappeared from the patriarch's gaze.

Reassured, Abraham returned to his tent. It was impossible that Sodom did not contain ten pure hearts. The city was saved! Then the hand of the Shaddai would turn away from those marked with the seal of his alliance, and by now, Lot and Naphis must already be circumcised.

He took his meal and went to sleep appeased. In his dreams he saw Naphis advancing with Radja, the young bride, and he imposed his hands on them to bless them. Then he perceived, in the depths of the sky, a luminous point that descended toward him, always increasing and scintillating more brightly. It grew into a nimbus at the center of which a newborn was resplendent. A blazing rain suddenly fell, each drop of which expanded into a new aureole, from which a child emerged, and gave birth itself to other similar globes, always multiplied . . .

He awoke, and, seeing Sara beside him, he remembered the Lord's promise. He approached her.

"What are you thinking, my Lord?" she murmured. "You're forgetting the years that have passed over my head, whitening my hair and sweeping away my beauty with the outrage of wrinkles."

"Don't attempt to fathom the judgments of God. My semen will germinate in your entrails by virtue of the fecundation of Elohim. Don't laugh! The Almighty has reproached my doubt and has given the son to whom you will give birth the name of Izehaq."

Abraham took Sara in his arms. She shuddered, and murmured: "I have conceived."

XIII

CURBED by his day's labor, Lot returned to Sodom slowly, followed by his wife. At the gate of the city he paused in order to draw breath, made his ablutions in the running water of a spring and bathed his forehead, burned by the sun, in the cool air poured forth by the bushy foliage of turpentine trees.

His donkey, laden with fruits and provender, was browsing the flavorsome grass, causing the ripe peaches to roll in its basket, as appetizing under their down as the cheek of a virgin under kisses; pomegranates laughed through their peel like living lips; enormous lemons with coppery tints and clusters of dates spread out in golden drops. In an earthenware jar, the pure honey of the bees of Arba oscillated slowly, and two inflated wineskins, which swayed in providing a counter-weight, contained the best wine of the harvest.

The Hebrew had spared no effort in order to honor his guest. He had understood Abram's thought and was thinking about the imminent wedding; his desire anticipated that of the patriarch; privately, he wondered: Radja or Zogar?

Radja was more superb, Zogar more gracious. Which would be Naphis' elect? The father had a happy smile. He would give him the elder first, and later the younger, Radja as soon as tomorrow, and once she was a mother, Naphis would find a virgin again in Zogar.

Lot got up and summoned his wife, who was dozing. He had picked up the tether of his donkey and was about to set forth again when two men approached the spring. Their faces emanated an aureole of light, in the bosom of which their supernatural beauty blossomed.

Struck by a religious dread, the patriarch advanced to meet the travelers and prostrated himself on the ground.

"Strangers, you whom my feeble eyes cannot contemplate without being dazzled and who are revealing yourselves to me as envoys of the celestial regions, honor your servant by eating at his table and sleeping under his roof. Attract divine benedictions upon him and upon his house by leaving the trace of your benevolent passage there."

The travelers lifted him up and said to him: "Who are you?"

"I am Lot, son of Harran, nephew of Abram, the Hebrew whose tents shelter beneath the oak of Mamré; and this," he added, indicating his wife, inclined a few paces behind him, "is the wife of your humble slave."

"Lot, hear through our mouth the voice of Elohim, who has sent us to you to transmit his commandments: you must be circumcised in your flesh before the sun has set behind the mountains twice more, along with the males of your family and the males among your servants."

"Praise be to Elohim in his will! I will submit to his orders. I render him thanks for having asked something of my humility. But come with me, Lords; consecrate my dwelling with your august presence."

"No," replied one of the divine messengers; "we have transmitted our message to you; our mission with regard to you is concluded; another is summoning us. We shall not enter your dwelling and will remain in the street."

"Do not inflict that affront on one faithful to the Almighty," Lot implored. "Do not scorn his hospitality. Lords; deign to follow me."

The travelers smiled and set forth, preceding the Hebrew, and stopped on the threshold of his house.

The patriarch, surprised, was asking them whether they had been to Sodom before, and whether he was known to them, when they interrupted him.

"One who has the gaze of Elohim in his eyes sees everything and knows everything; robust faith is not astonished."

Lot bowed, kissed the feet of his guests and conducted them to the porphyry bath. He purified them himself of the dust of the road, and then rubbed their limbs with cinnamon and smoothed their beard and their hair, which he anointed with grease and powdered with incense.

His wife and his daughters applied themselves to the preparation of the meal and served it to the strangers, who wanted Lot to take his place between them.

The Hebrew was worried by the absence of Naphis, and questioned his daughters. He had gone out shortly before the ninth hour of the day and had not returned to the palace. He had taken his traveling garments.

That detail troubled Lot. Had Naphis left Sodom? No! He would not have forgotten his duties to the extent of departing without taking his leave of the patriarch and asking whether he had any messages for Abram. Unless . . . What had happened in his absence? He interrogated his children, and learned nothing. Undoubtedly Naphis had gone astray in the maze of the city streets.

He sent his servants to search for the young man. Then he had beds prepared with his softest fleeces, his finest linen sheets; he conducted his guests to them, inviting them to take their repose there.

He could not sleep. His eyes, fixed on the sand-glass, watched the hours go past, interminably; his ears, listening to the sounds of the street, looked out for footsteps. At each closure of the door he shivered. One by one the slaves returned, without any news . . .

And Naphis did not return . . .

The inhabitants of Sodom had perceived the two sublime travelers as they passed by; some had followed them and had seen them enter the Hebrew's dwelling. Their superhuman beauty had dazzled the eyes, troubled the senses and awakened covetousness. The news of their arrival had been propagated from mouth to mouth, circulating in the streets, emptying the houses and accumulating at the crossroads. From all points of the city groups converged on Lot's palace; the assembly grew incessantly, becoming a crowd, massing and overflowing in more urgent waves, turbulent with impatience, ardent with curiosity and growling with lust.

They came from all over the city: squares, avenues, back-streets and doorways vomited a human lava swelling its lusts with an irresistible pressure, in an insatiable incandescence. Soon, the entire population was flowing, the men panting with bestiality, the women avid for fornication, and even the children, whose obscene temptations were already in search of sensuality.

The rumbling murmur of the crowd burst forth in furious vociferations and yapping clamors, mingled with the shrill notes of infantile voices. Hanging on to garments, climbing on to shoulders, the children seemed more avid than the adults, squinting their vicious eyes, in which a ferocious and unhealthy curiosity shone.

The old men were not the least ardent. Their senile appetites caught fire with a renewal of youth at the hope of the marvelous prey offered to their libidinousness.

From time to time, an overloaded man shook off the human cluster accumulated on his shoulders. The crowd was so dense that the dislodged individuals fell on the neighboring heads and clung on there, clawing and biting. Everyone was excited by the license of speech, which corroborated the lubricity of gestures. The entire multitude was shaken by the same frisson, breathing the same eroticism . . . and a heavy atmosphere, saturated with bestial exhalations and goatish reeks reigned, filling the lungs with its filthy prurience.

The disseminated cries melted into a single furious and thunderous clamor, to which fists beat time, hammering wildly on the Hebrew's door.

Noeph arrived, escorted by his band of libertines; he stimulated the passions of the populace, belching obscenities and blasphemies. Lifting up the tunics of women and children, stirring the crapulous vices of the mass by means of the exhibition of those nudities, ripe for the young people, scarcely formed for the old men. He delivered himself to the most shameless extravagances, displayed his virility and simulated, pressing against backs, an execrable coupling. And everyone applauded him, fêted him and recognized him as a leader.

Abimael and his cohanim, scarcely recovered from their orgiastic day, had come running, staggering drunkenly, accompanied by their ordinary ephebes. Even Bara, in spite of the gratitude that he owed to the Hebrew, had allowed himself to be drawn by the concupiscence of his concubines and his favorites. He had observed the bacchanal, half-dissimulated by the foliage of a nearby terrace, and, after his temporary repugnance, was now passionate for the strangers who were splendid to the extent of arousing an entire city. He amused himself by following the abject games and listening to the abominable speeches that polluted the gestures and the mouths of his people. He laughed, stirring the mud of his soul, wallowing in the abjection of his turpitude . . .

And his concubines clapped their hands, plucking flowers in order to throw them to the populace; one of them, leaning over too far, was precipitated; her fall crushed two men. There was an eddy in the crowd covering the square, which soon trampled the wounded and stifled their gasps of agony underfoot.

During the evening, Lot had heard the flood rising progressively, which was now battering his walls. At first he had not understood its purpose, but in the situation of anxiety that the inexplicable absence of Naphis put him, he was predisposed to be alarmed by it. Suddenly, a cry emerged from the din:

"The strangers!"

He understood, and went pale. He knew the bestial temperament of that people, which nothing could hold back when its appetites were in play. He had insisted on retaining his guests, and it was his guests who were menaced in his own home, by an entire city.

He was utterly terrified.

Blows of fists were succeeded by more violent impacts; stones clicked on the wood and the iron-work. The massive battens resisted, immovable in their solid stays. There was a pause, during which the first ranks, driven back, parted, stifling the rabble that was shoving them from behind . . . and then a silence . . . followed by a dull crack that shook the planks. A second succeeded it, dis-jointing the timbers. Swung by a hundred arms, a heavy beam rebounded from the portal, causing the wood to groan, flexing the planks and causing the hinges to screech.

Lot sensed the gravity of the moment. In the face of the inevitable danger he recovered his calmness and strength. Imposing silence on his frightened slaves, who were clinging to him in order to hold him back, driving them away with a gesture, he opened the door wide, went out and closed it behind him.

Bare-headed on the threshold, his forehead high, he braved the mob, dominating it. Beneath the snowy tangle of his eyebrows, his menacing gaze sparkled, so imperious that the horde recoiled, and its ranks opened before him as if driven back by a mysterious force. His arms, folded over his chest, over which a long white beard dangled, suddenly extended, hovering over the people and commanding silence . . .

He took two steps forward and asked:

"What do you want?"

His majestic attitude imposed upon the populace. The wild beast bowed down under the will of its tamer. Perhaps the multitude was about to withdraw before the august old man, when an eddy upset it; Noeph broke through the living wall and, sneering at the patriarch, cried in an arrogant voice:

"The men you received this evening are beautiful; we want them."

"You want them!"

"We want them in order to enjoy them!"

Lot stared at the debauchee and spat on the ground.

But Noeph had awakened the filthy instincts of the rabble, more furious in its revived liberation, as a torrent is after the resistance of a dike that its flood has finally demolished, and a cacophony of imprecations thundered:

"We want them! We want them!"

With the gestures of the possessed, and epileptic contortions, the circle tightened, pressing Lot, whose voice still dominated the tumult:

"Brothers, I address myself to your honor. Those men are my guests; they entered my house as into an inviolable sanctuary. You would not want foreign nations to say that the people of Sodom scorned the sacred laws of hospitality . . ."

In its ferocious obstinacy, maddened by brutal desire, the crowd howled:

"We want those men!"

Lot went on:

"Friends, don't yield to a shameful passion; don't give yourselves to execrable fornications reproved by divine and human laws . . ."

Abimael, followed by his cortege, had reached the first rank; he interrupted the patriarch:

"We need them! The stars have declared it! Such is the will of Nabou!"

An enthusiastic acclamation saluted these words; everyone, stamping their feet with joy, applauded frantically. Nabou would deliver the strangers to the appetites of his people.

The Hebrew made a supreme effort.

"The god of Abram, who has avenged Sodom against the Elamites, who has rendered you your liberty and your wealth, forbids you! You know whether I am devoted to you, ingrates! My uncle, in fighting for Sodom did it for me. Well, then, I will do more for you. I have for daughters two virgins, two flowers of beauty and youth. You

know them? I give them to you, they are yours
. . . but do not outrage my honorable old age by
abusing my guests; do not soil yourselves with a
sacrilegious sin!"

Noeph drew closer, face to face, his eyes wild
and his fists clenched.

"Get away!" he said, with a violent gesture. "A
foreigner you came, a foreigner you still are. What
right have you to institute yourself as our judge in
our own home? Get back, obey, yield those men
to us or we will deliver you to the children in order
to teach them pleasure on your old carcass!"

Lot raised his arms toward the heavens and
stiffened them over Noeph.

"Be accursed, son of a sow, excrement of adul-
tery! A curse on you, on yours and your race!"

And, turning his head away in disgust, he spat
over his shoulder.

Noeph bore his impious hand to the patriarch's
beard, shook his head sniggering, and then, with
a brutal twist of the wrist, knocked him down on
the threshold of his own palace.

The paroxysm of the mob rushed freely over
the last crumbled dike; the body of the Hebrew
felt the first bruises of the crush beneath the trampling of the crowd.

The door opened; the angels of God appeared,
so flamboyant in their glory that the dazzled eyes
of the multitude were struck with blindness.

The angels lifted Lot up, carried him inside and closed the door again, which the impotent fury of the crowd could not rediscover.

Invectives, howls, the shrill wails of women and children and the roaring blasphemies of men burst forth in a bacchanal that their disappointment vomited more wrathfully. Their insensate exasperation gave rise to bloody brawls; fists lashed out at random, fingernails clawed, teeth bit, growls of hatred were mingled with strident cries of pain. Then the overflowing madness of the multitude degenerated into lubricious scenes and frightful couplings; a wind of lust passed over the crowd, which was no longer anything but a flock of fornicating goats . . .

Inside the palace, Lot and his saviors were surrounded by the women, from whom fear extracted sobs. They kissed their knees, holding out their suppliant hands.

Elohim's envoys spoke:

"Man of good, take with you your wife, your daughters and those whom you love. Sodom is condemned. The cry of its abominations has risen ever higher toward the Lord; its corruption has arrived at its culmination; the mud of iniquity has overflowed. The Shaddai has sent us to annihilate it in a pitiless cataclysm. Not one stone will remain atop another; the very place will be submerged by a sinister lake, which will keep its unfathomable secret."

Lot resisted.

"Naphis, Abram's adopted child, had been confided to my hearth; at this moment he is absent from my dwelling. Could I dare to reappear before my uncle without the cherished son of his old age, without the one who, alone, gives him the joys of paternity? I am a father, Lords! Could I dare to raise my forehead to the daylight if I abandon my guest? Could you, angels of God, counsel me to fail in the duties of hospitality? Is it for me, who has received from you the seal of Elohim, to buckle? I shall stay until Naphis returns. I shall save him with me or perish with him. I have spoken!"

"The ways of the Almighty are unfathomable," pronounced one of the messengers. "Cease to lament for the brother of your father; at this hour, in spite of her sterile youth, Sara, in her fecund old age, feels the flesh and blood of Abraham quivering in the depths of her entrails. Elohim is procreating a son for him. We have the mission to save you; we are saving you."

With an inflexible grip, the hands of the envoys of Heaven gripped the patriarch's arm. They pushed the Hebrew's wife and daughters ahead of them and went out through a hidden postern.

Lot wept!

Outside the walls the first of the Angels spoke:

"March straight ahead of you without looking back; do not stop and have no fear; God will guide you and protect you. Anyone who stops walking or turns their head will perish, like the damned of Sodom."

"Lords," implored Lot, "since your servant has found grace in the eyes of Elohim, and, in conserving his life, the Almighty is showing him his greatest mercy, hear my prayer. I am old; my steps are heavy and unsteady; my wife and my daughters have delicate feet unaccustomed to long marches. Before us is Bala, which is a very small town; suffer that we seek refuge there and that God will spare it."

"Your prayer is granted. Make haste. Celestial vengeance will break its craters before you have found shelter in that town which, because of its smallness, will henceforth be called Zo'har."

And the Angels, flying in the ether, pushed clouds of fire over Sodom.

XIV

NIGHT descended on the temple, wadded it with silence and filled it with darkness. Somber clouds, still thickening, were rising from the horizon, englobing the sky, accumulating menacingly. Their air, overladen with tempests, stagnated heavily, oppressing breasts and burning foreheads. The acrid odors of the fête, surviving the daylight, misted the night.

Maheleth, still inanimate, reposed on her couch alone. Basemath was on watch beside her. Naphis, thrown into a profound cellar, had heard the grille fall back heavily above him with a sinister vibration, the clink of chains and the grating of padlocks; then the footsteps of his jailers faded, dying away in the distance, abandoning him to the terror of the sepulcher in which he had been buried alive.

The Cohanim, informed of the presence of the marvelous guests sheltered by the son of Harran, had rushed toward that new prey in the wake of the assembled populace.

Drawn by the general current, the guards and servants had deserted their posts; all of them, stirred by the same itch, were laying siege to the Hebrew's abode . . .

On emerging from her long faint, the daughter of Abimael preserved a clear vision of the scene of abomination. Her thoughts went straight to Naphis. What fate was reserved for him?

She found herself alone with Basemath, told her to come closer and then burst into tears on the bosom of her faithful nurse.

She learned that her beloved was imprisoned in the catacombs of the temple of Nabou, destined for the lusts of the priestly fornicators.

He was alive! But if he had to live thus, death was better! It was necessary to liberate him and flee with him.

How? Her thought was lost in that contemplation; but her will was extended toward that sole objective, fixedly and tenaciously. How? She would find a way . . .

"Basemath! Basemath!" she cried, illuminated by a hope. "Who is the guardian of the dungeons?"

"Magog, Princess," replied the nurse, mechanically; then she stood up abruptly, slapped her forehead, and cried: "I understand!"

"Yes, you've understood me. Magog is a drunkard. The banqueting hall must be open. Go find the jailer, talk to him about the wines and liqueurs that are crowding the tables; stimulate his vice, offer to go and savor them with him. He only wants to be convinced. There, get him drunk; and when torpor seals his eyelids, steal his keys, come back, and guide me to the dungeons."

"I will attempt anything for you, my princess."

"Kiss me, Basemath. I am no longer the daughter of the man who wanted to soil me. Has he not denied me himself? My mother is dead; you are my mother!"

"My child!" sobbed the old nurse, melting her heart in a kiss . . .

In the depths of his prison, Naphis was thinking. After an explosion of rage he had sunk into a collapse of his entire being. His burning forehead was suffering from its branding; he applied it, dolorously, to the stone of the walls in order to cool the burning wound . . . and he thought!

It was over then! The trap extended by the nymphomaniac girls would cost him his fiancée, cost him his life and doom his amour! Stigmatized by the sign of Nabou, he would be the plaything of the lubricity of the cohanim, those filthy men. He, the proud victor, the hero of Hoba, whose name ought to be inscribed in streaks of terror in the memory of the Elamites, was no longer anything but a prostitute!

But he suppressed the revolt that was seething within him, in order only to think about the unfortunate Maheleth, a captive, condemned to rape by her father or the ignoble coupling of the vile Noeph . . . perhaps both those pollutions, which doubtless also awaited him. Oh, how he was suffering . . . to know that his Beloved was threatened and to be impotent . . . ! An atrocious jealousy clawed his heart . . . He saw again the insensate spectacles that he had surprised, the disgusting abjection of those vile and libidinous priests, their crapulous lips drooling over the immaculate flesh of the one whom amour made his, and her, tied up and broken, subject to their leprous contact . . . and he, perhaps alongside her, condemned to the same mistreatment and to contemplate the pollution of the object of his adoration! He would have liked to die, but not to leave his fiancée alive in the lascivious hands of her torturers. At that moment he would have been thankful for the death of Maheleth, for he would also have been able to die!

But he did not want to die while he knew that she was alive. In order to attempt an escape, although he judged it to be impossible, he rolled against the grille, curling himself up. There he wore away his bonds by means of a relentless friction. The ropes were gradually shredded; he redoubled his ardor. When the last thread yielded he got up, reaffirmed by a glimmer of hope. Once the liberty of his limbs was recovered, his self-confidence returned; it seemed to him to be the pledge of true liberty, that of the woods, the air and the great blue sky.

He sounded his dungeon, groping. The smooth walls, coated with bitumen, offered no fissures or grooves; the enormous grilles were framed in deep ruts, strongly sealed, unbreakable; they were so narrowly forged that his hand could not penetrate between their bars. He shook them wrathfully, multiplying tenfold in that effort the vigor that had once enabled him to strangle a wild beast between his fingers, but he could not succeed in imparting a vibration to them. Then his bloodied hands were raised for a supreme appeal, his knees flexed and his voice wept:

"Eloi, Eloi, lama sabachthani!" [1]

✳

The darkness is punctured by a distant spark; it draws nearer, vacillating and gradually dilating. Naphis, his eyes fixed, holding his breath, the blood buzzing in his temples, sees it grow, coming toward him . . .

Two phantoms glide through the penumbra . . . keys grate in the massive lock; the bars are unclenched, the bolts screech, the portcullis opens . . . Maheleth is in Naphis' arms!

Superb embrace, in which both have rediscovered strength and faith; unbreakable bonds that make them powerful and invincible; united with one another, they can brave the universe, they are masters of life!

Basemath has left them alone; she has gone to reconnoiter the exit from the subterrains and to prepare the escape.

Finally, Maheleth's mouth opens and her oppressed voice murmurs: "Come, my beloved; let us flee this accursed place and be happy!"

---

1 The opening words of the twenty-second psalm, repeated by Jesus on the cross: "My God, My God, why has thou forsaken me?"

"Oh, let me adore your eyes, hearths of my light; allow my heart to beat upon your breast, the refuge of my head; give me your lips, the source of my life . . . Maheleth, our amour laughs at the darkness, it illuminates my dungeon."

"I love you," the virgin sighs.

Their lips unite . . .

Then from the depths of the clouds, lightning springs; a bellowing clamor rolls through space, tearing the darkness, filling the east and the west with its formidable echoes.

Shaddai spoke:

"The cry of the iniquities of Sodom has grown all the way to my hearth, you who love one another in the law of the Lord!"

Everything fell silent. In the universal calm of the night the sound of a kiss passed . . .

Lightning flashes were detonated in the atmosphere; the voice spoke again:

"Children, your amour smiles at the Almighty; his wrath will fall upon the city of fornicators; flee, for the hour is nigh!"

Silence reigned . . . Maheleth's veil had fallen; through the night, the beating of two hearts rose in union . . .

✳

The thunder burst forth again.

"Flee, time is passing!"

Only a double sigh rose up in the ether; the lovers only heard the sobs drunk by their lips upon their lips . . . they were united forever!

A dense, livid, sulfurous cloud covers Sodom; fantastic lightning-bolts spring from its flanks; the craters of the firmament open their ardent mouths; fire falls from the sky, as if the stars were rushing upon the earth in a sudden collapse. Roars rumble below among the din of strident squalls; in a crackle of hail the rain of fire descends on domes, biting and eviscerating roofs, stones fuse, bursting in the racket of their deflagrations. Trees twist and totter, knotting together in the blazing stream; vaults of bitumen melt, dripping incandescent lava; the ground trembles and cracks; edifices oscillate on their bases and collapse. Sodom burns in a nauseating, acrid smoke streaked by tongues of flame . . . A cry rises up, filling the city with its lugubrious crescendo; the howls trail off in desperate gasps . . .

Swooning, Naphis murmured: "Sustain me with flowers, fortify me with fruits, for I am languid with amour . . .

And Maheleth perfumed his lips with kisses, slaked his thirst from the spring of her nipples . . .

A swarming crowd rushes out of the houses; ferociously, everyone attempts to cleave a passage; frightened mothers tear newborns from their breast and throw them away, in order to flee more freely; in the blocked streets the tide rises; people are stifling; living clusters build up, feet trampling old men, women and children; the strong crush the weak. Under the gigantic pressure the human pyramid collapses, soon covered by another, and the pile accumulates, tangled, swollen, howls and thrashes dementedly, contorting in impotent somersaults, while the red flood falls and penetrates, setting the living brazier aflame.

The sizzling of flesh fills the atmosphere with the stink of burning fat; blood and entrails overflow from split bodies, fuming and volatilizing; human scoria emerge amid the broth of the igneous tide, dissolve therein and sink . . . and the tide is still growing . . .

No more cries . . . but gasps, gurgling hiccups, the crackle of roasting meat, blistering and bursting . . . and blue sulfurous tongues run over the furnace . . .

*

In the depths of his dungeon, Naphis sighed:

"Don't wake up, soul of my soul; let your forehead repose on my breast; you are mine forever!"

In a whisper as soft as the kiss of a wave dying on the strand, Maheleth stammered:

"I belong to my beloved, and his heart is turned toward me."

With a languid gesture her arms knotted themselves around Naphis' neck, and her lips sought his caresses . . .

And her lover, renascent in his delights, leaned her against his heart again . . .

*

Red and bellowing, the torrent of lava is precipitated over the paving stones of the temple; its tide rises, still rising, carrying away enormous steles and squat idols; with shrill hisses it licks the walls; with its enraged impacts it shakes, undermines and uproots their granite ramparts; sections of wall and colonnades crumble, splashing the air with fulgurant spray; then a furious pressure rips up the paving stones and plunges into the subterrain, pouring into its depths, roaring, and carrying away the stone bed on which the lovers are spelling out their amour, like an ice-floe . . .

In one another's arms, their eyes seeing nothing but their smiles, they float away on the ocean of fire, linked by an immutable embrace, welded together by an inexhaustible desire . . .

Finally, the furnace devours their floating couch, attains them, absorbs them . . . As they sink into the incandescent flow, they drink a flame that is refreshing for them by comparison with their kisses . . .

A frisson runs over the lava . . . The breath of Elohim passes, carrying away two souls from their apotheosis of Amour toward Eternity!

Aix-en-Provence, 1885.
Villa della Rocca, Ajaccio, 1888.

A PARTIAL LIST OF SNUGGLY BOOKS

G. ALBERT AURIER *Elsewhere and Other Stories*
S. HENRY BERTHOUD *Misanthropic Tales*
LÉON BLOY *The Desperate Man*
LÉON BLOY *The Tarantulas' Parlor and Other Unkind Tales*
ÉLÉMIR BOURGES *The Twilight of the Gods*
CYRIEL BUYSSE *The Aunts*
JAMES CHAMPAGNE *Harlem Smoke*
FÉLICIEN CHAMPSAUR *The Latin Orgy*
BRENDAN CONNELL *Clark*
BRENDAN CONNELL *Unofficial History of Pi Wei*
RAFAELA CONTRERAS *The Turquoise Ring and Other Stories*
ADOLFO COUVE *When I Think of My Missing Head*
QUENTIN S. CRISP *Aiaigasa*
LADY DILKE *The Outcast Spirit and Other Stories*
CATHERINE DOUSTEYSSIER-KHOZE
    The Beauty of the Death Cap
ÉDOUARD DUJARDIN *Hauntings*
BERIT ELLINGSEN *Now We Can See the Moon*
ERCKMANN-CHATRIAN *A Malediction*
ENRIQUE GÓMEZ CARRILLO *Sentimental Stories*
EDMOND AND JULES DE GONCOURT *Manette Salomon*
REMY DE GOURMONT *From a Faraway Land*
GUIDO GOZZANO *Alcina and Other Stories*
EDWARD HERON-ALLEN *The Complete Shorter Fiction*
RHYS HUGHES *Cloud Farming in Wales*
J.-K. HUYSMANS *The Crowds of Lourdes*
J.-K. HUYSMANS *Knapsacks*
COLIN INSOLE *Valerie and Other Stories*
JUSTIN ISIS *Pleasant Tales II*
JUSTIN ISIS AND DANIEL CORRICK (editors)
    Drowning in Beauty: The Neo-Decadent Anthology

CPSIA information can be obtained
at www.ICGtesting.com
Printed in the USA
LVHW030623281220
675178LV00001BA/34

9 781645 250579